How I Overcame Middle School

Written by

Vaniece Washington

This book is a work of fiction. Names, characters, places, and incidents are the product of the author's imagination or are used fictitiously. Any resemblance to actual events, locales, or persons, living or dead, is coincidental.

For a copy of my book, please contact:

Melvina Washington at

Sweet Thangs Mom Publishing LLC

856-924-0583

Sweetthangsmom@gmail.com

ISBN: 978-1-7359449-0-6 (paperback)

ISBN: 978-1-7359449-2-0 (ebook)

First Edition: October 2020

Instagram: @iamvaniece

Facebook: Vaniece Washington

Resources and Statistics

- According to statistics, 1 out of 5 kids report being bullied

https://www.pacer.org/bullying/resources/stats.asp

- There are about 4,400 deaths by suicide amongst young people per year. As it is the third leading cause of deaths among youth

http://www.bullyingstatistics.org/content/bullying-and-suicide.html

- Types of bullying include

1. Physical bullying (can cause short term or long term damage)
2. Verbal bullying; while it may start off harmless, it may escalate.
3. Social bullying (aka covert bullying): This can be hard to recognize because it usually takes place behind the victim's back. It means to humiliate or cause harm to someone's reputation or social acceptance.
4. Cyber bullying (can be overt or covert, can happen in public or private)

https://www.ncab.org.au/bullying-advice/bullying-for-parents/types-of-bullying/

The King James Bible; Spiritual Reference.

About the Author

Vaniece Washington, is a senior at Paul VI High School in New Jersey. She plans on attending college in the Fall of 2021. Vaniece began writing books at the age of 10. She is the only child and lives in New Jersey with her parents. Vaniece enjoys playing the piano, singing, and writing stories. Vaniece realized at an early age the severity of bullying amongst tweens and teens as well as the various types of bullying. Vaniece had some of her own challenges that prompt her to write this book. She realized there was a place she could go to overcome those challenges. She owes it all to her Lord and Savior Jesus Christ.

The contents of this book is relateable to many teenagers attending Middle School. At one point or another you were the bully, or you were the one being bullied, you observed someone being bullied or you stood up for someone being bullied. Who are you in this intriguing book?

Vaniece is already working on the sequel to How I got over Middle School and hopes to be a #1 best selling author one day.

Dedication

This book is dedicated to anyone who has faced the hardships of bullying of any level of severity or anyone who is in need of encouragement.

Acknowledgement

First off, I would like to give the glory and honor to my Lord and Savior Jesus Christ for His constant lovingkindness, tender mercy and forgiveness even when I didn't deserve it. If it had not been for God on my side, I would not have been able to conquer the challenges that I faced in life. I am thankful for the talent and ability to write stories. Second, I would like to thank my mom and dad for giving me good advice when it was needed and for teaching me how to conduct myself as a young Christian black woman. Next, I would like to thank my grandparents for showering their only grandbaby with as much love as their hearts can hold. The amount of memories that we shared over the years will most definitely be some of the best times of my life. I have to give thanks to my Uncle Bill, who is the greatest biblical teacher you could ever imagine. God has given him the ability to teach the bible incorporated with love and for that I am grateful. Finally, I would like to thank my entire family and friends who showed me love.

TABLE OF CONTENTS

Chapter 1: Room 132

My name is Autumn Johnson, and I'm 13 years old.

My parents' names are Robert and Michelle Johnson. I have 3 sisters: Nikki, Jade and Summer. Nikki is 9, Jade is 4 and Summer is only 1 year old. My family and I used to live in Phoenix, Arizona, but we just moved to Miami, Florida. It's my first day of school and I'm so excited, but a little bit nervous. I brushed my teeth, got dressed and then went into the living room. As I was walking out the door, my mom called me.

"Wait, Autumn. Give your mother a kiss goodbye first!" She yelled.

"Mom, I'm getting way too old for this." I said.

"Oh puh-lease. You just turned 13 like 3 months ago." Said Nikki.

"Which means I'm a teenager now. Mom, I have to go, I'm going to be late." I said.

"So, are you excited about school so far?" Mom asked.

"I'm not so sure. I am really excited, but I'm also nervous. What do you think the kids are like here?" I asked.

"I'm sure it'll be all fine, sweetie. Now come here and give me a kiss!"

"Mom!"

"Ok. Then can I at least have a goodbye hug?"

"Ok, fine." I gave her a hug and she kissed my forehead anyway.

"Mom!" I yelled . My mom laughed at me.

"See you later, baby." Said mom.

"Bye!" I said, walking out of the door.

Once I got to school, it was so big, and I got super nervous. I went inside and went straight to the main office, as instructed, and got all the textbooks for my classes, and then went to go put them in my locker. I met the principal while I was there, too. He seemed pretty cool.

As I was walking down the hallway, I bumped into a boy and dropped all my books that I had. I quickly picked up all my books, but as I went to grab the last book, another hand met mine. I looked up and saw the cutest boy I have ever seen in my life. I stared into his eyes and it was like I was being hypnotized.

"Hey, need some help?" He asked, as I was finally snapping out of it.

"Ummm, Yeah. I guess." I mumbled. We both stood up.

"You must be new here. What's your name?" He asked. I stared into his eyes, unaware that he even asked me a question. He waved in my face.

"Umm, hellloooo?" He said.

"Oh, umm." I muttered. I was finally able to talk again, but I almost wish I weren't after I said this.

"Umm. I'm Autumn Marie Johnson. But most people don't call me Marie. Marie is my middle name. I go by Autumn. But you can call me whatever you want. OK, YOU TALK NOW...." I laughed, nervously. He chuckled awkwardly.

"I'm Jackson." He said. The bell rang. That meant breakfast in the cafeteria was being served.

"See you later?" He asked.

"Umm, ok. Buh-bye. See ya. Toodles! Adios!" I could not believe I was still going; he was long gone already. I even let myself go as far as "adios," what's the matter with me? I rolled my eyes at myself and walked away.

As I walked to the cafeteria, there were four girls standing by the register staring at me disapprovingly. I decided to kill them with kindness by smiling at them. Two of them gave me a dirty look and the other two looked me up and down. I looked away and began walking off.

"Looks like there's a new girl in town." Said one of the girls as I walked by.

"Wow! Look at that purse! Where did you get it? The dollar store?" One of them asked. Then they all stood around laughing at me, so I just walked away. I sat down at an empty table. When I put my tray down two more girls came and sat with me.

"You must be new here!" Said one of the girls.

"What's your name?" Said the other girl.

"I'm Autumn." I said.

"I'm Serenity." Said one of the girls.

"And I'm Lauren." Said the other girl. Serenity and Lauren saw the girls in the corner staring and laughing.

"Um, who are they?" I asked.

"That's Ivey! She's the most popular girl in school." Said Serenity.

"And those are her friends Sandra, Leah, and Zoey. Leah is Ivey's best friend, they do almost everything together. Zoey is the best at roasting people. And Sandra, well, she's not the sharpest tool in the box." Said Lauren.

“Either way, you do *not* want to mess with them.” Said Serenity.

“Not that I want to, but what’ll happen?” I asked.

“That’s just the thing! You never know what that girl is up to. She’s unpredictable!” Said Lauren. Soon Ivey and the girls came up to us.

“Umm, excuse you! Are you talking about me?” Asked Ivey. Serenity and Lauren both looked away and didn’t say anything. I stared at her.

“Hello! Can you not hear me talking to you?!” She demanded.

“I think she’s ignoring you.” Said Sandra.

“Wow, really? I didn’t notice! Sandra, why do you have to be so stupid?” Asked Ivey.

“Anyway, I saw you flirting with my boyfriend!” She continued.

“Your boyfriend? Who’s that?” I asked.

“Jackson Smith! You were flirting with him!” She said.

“What? No! He was helping me pick up my books that I dropped!”

“Well, I’m warning you! You had better stay away from Jackson, or else we’re going to have a problem.” Said Ivey. I scoffed.

“Is that supposed to be a threat?” I asked.

“No, sweetie.... It’s a promise.” Said Ivey, intimidatingly.

“I doubt he even likes you anyway! I mean, just look in the mirror. You really need to put on some makeup. You’re ugly!” Said Zoey. Then they all laughed and walked away.

“I hate her so much!” Said Serenity, rolling her eyes.

“I know right! She’s so mean to everyone!” Said Lauren. Looks like this girl’s going to be a problem for me. I rolled my eyes.

"This is going to be a *long* year." I said, annoyed.

"So, Autumn, right?" Asked Serenity, trying to remember my name.

"Yep!"

"Autumn, where are you from?"

"I'm from Arizona." They both shuddered.

"Imagine how hot it is over there." Said Lauren.

"Yeah, it is really hot in Arizona. Especially in mid-July. We once actually fried an egg on the roof!" I said. They both stared at me with their mouths open.

"Oh, my gosh. I thought that was just a saying!" Said Lauren.

"Not in Arizona!" I said. The 3 of us laughed.

"Well, I hope you and your family like it here." Said Serenity.

"It's definitely rainier here." I said, jokingly. We laughed again.

"But so far I really do like it in Florida. There's a lake right by my house and my sisters and I can go swimming in it."

"Wow, that sounds fun!" Said Serenity.

"Just be careful of all the crabs that hang out along the bay. They're *way* meaner than the regular crabs.... They're Florida crabs!" Said Lauren. We laughed again. Then the bell rang, which meant it was time for home room.

"Autumn. What's your home room?" Said Serenity.

"I'm in room 132."

"Hey, then I'm right next to you! I can just walk you down there."

"Thanks!"

"See you later!" Said Lauren, walking away.

"Byeeee!" We both said as she walked away. Serenity and I walked down to my home room.

"And here it is, room 132."

"Thanks, Serenity." I said.

"No problem. Also, I'm right next door, so just let me know if you need help with anything." She said, walking into her home room.

"Ok, see you later!" I said.

"Byeee!" She said, walking in. Wow, I've already made two friends on my first day. So far, I think I might like it here.

Chapter 2: Classes

Once I got to first period, which was AP English, I sat in the seat in the middle of the class.

"Ok, class! Take your seats! It looks like we have a new student. Autumn Johnson, why don't you stand up and introduce yourself?" Said Ms. Anderson. I stood up. I got nervous because everyone turned to look at me.

"I'm Autumn Johnson, and I'm 13 years old." I said, in a shy way. I sat down super quick.

"Um, can you say a bit more about yourself, like how are you enjoying Miami so far?" She asked.

"So far, I really like it here! There's a lake right by my house so my sisters and I can go swimming whenever we want." I said.

"Too bad you don't have a house with an actual pool and hot tub! Only you would want to swim around in dirty lake water." Yelled out Ivey. Then the whole class laughed, so I sat down again.

"Is that all you want to share, Autumn?" Asked Ms. Anderson.

"That's probably the only thing she *can* talk about, she's not special anyway!" Said Ivey.

Everyone laughed again. I put my head down on the desk. A few minutes later someone tapped my shoulder. I looked up and turned around, and it was Jackson sitting behind me! I didn't even realize he was in this class. I was getting nervous about what he was about to say.

"Don't listen to Ivey, she's just mean." He said. I smiled.

"Thanks." I said, turning back around.

A couple of hours later, was 3rd period, which was science. Which is great because I love science! I walked into class and the first person I saw was Ivey and her friend Zoey. I just hope they don't spoil science for me. I walked in and sat down in the front. The teacher walked up to me.

"Hello, you must be new. My name is Ms. Dobbins." She said.

"I'm Autumn Johnson!" I said. She shook my hand.

"It's very nice to meet you, sweetie." She said. As she walked away, Ivey and Zoey walked up.

"You know Autumn, this is an accelerated science class. Think it might be too much of a challenge for you?" Said Ivey.

"Um, no. I was actually one of the students with the highest GPA at my previous school." I said. Zoey scoffed.

"Nerd." She laughed. She and Ivey laughed and then walked away. I rolled my eyes. Soon the bell rang and class started.

"Ok, class let's get started. We have a new student today: Autumn Johnson." Said Ms. Dobbins, motioning to me. The class slightly applauded.

"So Autumn, I hear you enjoy science!" She said.

"Oh, I love science! In fact, at my old school, I was one of the smartest kids in my science class." I bragged.

"Oh, really? I see you were in the delayed program." She said. Ivey and Zoey snickered behind me.

"Um, no. I was in the accelerated program actually. And I was one of the top ten in the entire school." I said.

"I'm assuming you were tenth." She said. Ivey and Zoey snickered again behind me. I raised up an eyebrow at her. She's supposed to be the teacher, not another one of the mean girls. I was actually the seventh, but I didn't want to talk back because I'd get in trouble.

"Ok, class. Pick a partner and get started on page 73 in your workbooks. Autumn, you can work by yourself for now. I'm assuming you haven't made any friends yet." She said, again. Ivey and Zoey snickered behind me again.

"Autumn can work with me!" Someone yelled across the room. I turned around and it was Serenity!

"Autumn. We have a volunteer." Said Ms. Dobbins.

"More like a friend." Said Serenity, walking up to my desk. I smiled.

"Ok, class. You guys have 15 minutes, get started." Said Ms. Dobbins. Serenity sat in the seat next to me.

"Thanks!" I said.

"No problem. And ignore Ms. Dobbins, she's miserable. And you know what they say right? 'Misery loves company'!" Said Serenity. Serenity and I chuckled. Ivey and Zoey stood up and stood behind us.

"Really, because I like her." Said Ivey, as we both turned around.

"Yeah, she's going to put you back in your place." Said Zoey, pointing in my face with her finger.

I wanted to say "Girl, if you don't get your nasty, stinking finger out of my face, I'll break it in half!", but I didn't. It's my first day! I didn't want to cause too much chaos. They both whipped their hair in my face and walked away.

Last period that day I had Study Hall. After the bell rang, the teacher went to the front of the class.

"Hello, class. My name is Mr. Lee. And I only say that because I see we have a new student: Autumn." He said, motioning to me. The class applauded lightly.

"Ok, so class is going to be like always. Study for a test or do homework. If you want to, you can quietly talk to a friend, but just be mindful of the other people around you. Ok, get started." He said. Mr. Lee seems really chill; I have a good feeling about him already. I got out some of my homework and started working on it for a while. After about 10 minutes, someone walked up to me. I looked up and it was Lauren, the girl I met at breakfast today.

"Hey, Lauren!" I said.

"Hey, Autumn. Whatcha working on?" She asked, sitting down next to me.

"French homework." I said.

"You take French?"

"Yep. But only because I've already taken Spanish since like 4th grade, and I'm basically already fluent in it. So, I took French so I could be trilingual!"

"Wow, that's impressive!" Lauren looked at my homework.

"Wow, that looks hard! I wouldn't be able to handle French." She said, laughing. She and I both laughed.

"So, how are you enjoying this school so far?"

"So far, I really like it here. You know, except for Ivey." Lauren looked shocked.

"Ivey? But I thought Ivey took mostly advanced courses." She said.

"Yeah, she's in my AP English class and in my accelerated science class." I said.

“You take accelerated science?!” She asked, even more shocked.

“Yep. Science is my favorite subject, and at my old school I was at the top of my class in science, so they put me in an accelerated course here.”

“I bet Ivey was really excited about that.” Said Lauren, sarcastically.

“Yeah, her little friend called me a nerd.” I said. Lauren and I both laughed. Another girl in front of us turned around.

“I’m sorry, but I couldn’t help but overhear. Were you guys just talking about Ivey Sanders?” She asked. Lauren and I both looked at each other. I guess Lauren didn’t recognize her either.

“Yes, who’s asking?” Said Lauren.

“My name is Tara. It’s nice to meet you.” She answered.

“Cool. I’m Lauren, and this is Autumn.” Said Lauren.

“The new girl?” Asked Tara.

“That’s me!” I said.

“Yeah. But anyway, if it’s one thing I know about Ivey Sanders, it’s that she does *not* like competition. She just always wants to be number 1.” Said Tara.

“Well, that’ll be real fun. She already hates me because I was talking to Jackson.” I chucked. Tara looked shocked.

“You talked to Jackson Smith?!” She asked.

“Yes. And why is everyone so impressed by that?” I asked.

“It’s just that Ivey and Jackson are dating, and just like I said earlier, Ivey does *not* like competition. So if I were you, I’d just stay away from Jackson.” Said Tara.

"Ok, class it's a little too loud in here, so I'm going to have to ask you guys to simmer down." Announced Mr. Lee.

"I'm going to finish my homework. Talk later?" I said to Tara.

"Yeah, sure. It was nice meeting you!" She said, turning around.

"You too!" I said. I looked back at Lauren.

"Well, she seems nice." I said.

"I'd just be careful around her, too. I've heard some not so good things about her." Said Lauren.

"Ok, I'll keep that in mind." I said. Lauren and I both worked on our homework until the final bell, then everyone got up and left.

I got out of school at 3:00. I start riding the bus tomorrow, so today I had to walk home. Once I got home, I walked in and walked into the kitchen to see my mom.

"Hey, mom!" I said. She turned around.

"Hi, Sweetie!" She said, walking up to hug me. We hugged each other.

"How was your first day of school?" She asked.

"Sort of a rollercoaster." I said.

"Well, tell me about it. Did you get all of your textbooks for the year? How were the kids there? How are the teachers?"

"Mom calm down! I just got home!" I said, chuckling.

"But overall, it was pretty good. I already made two friends." I said, again.

"Wow, already? Tell me about them."

"Their names are Serenity and Lauren. Serenity is in my science class and Lauren is in my study hall. Also, I met this other girl in my study hall named Tara, she seems pretty cool too."

"See? I told you it will be all fine."

"Yeah, but I also have trouble with some people."

"Trouble? What do you mean?"

"There's this guy I talked to and—" My mom interrupted me.

"Oooh." She said.

"There's nothing going on between us! Besides, he has a girlfriend. The most popular girl in school, her name's Ivey. She's the girl I have problems with." I said.

"Really?"

"Yeah. She already has a problem with me because she saw me talking to her boyfriend, Jackson."

"Oh, don't worry about her Sweetie. That's just how teenagers are."

"Well, I guess you're right."

"I'm sure you'll be fine, just ignore Ivey and focus on the support you have at school and at home."

"Ok. Thanks, mom!" I said. After that, I started telling my mom about my classes and my opinions on different teachers.

Chapter 3: Science

The next day, I rode the bus to school. The good thing is that Lauren, one of the girls I met yesterday, rides the bus with me. So at least I don't have to ride the bus alone.

When I arrived at school, I sat with Serenity and Lauren again for breakfast.

"Hey Autumn!" Said Serenity.

"Hey, guys!" I said, sitting down.

"So, how was your first day yesterday?" Asked Serenity.

"It was surprisingly good. Except for the classes I have with Ivey. She's in my English *and* science class." I said.

"Ooh. I feel bad for you." Said Serenity. We chuckled.

"Oh, well. At least we still have some classes together." Said Lauren.

"What classes do you take?" Asked Serenity.

"I take accelerated science, French, pre-Algebra, study hall, American History, AP English and art." I answered.

"Wow, you take a lot of hard courses!" Said Serenity.

"Thanks!" I said.

"I heard American History was hard!" Said Lauren.

"It doesn't seem that hard. But it's definitely a lot of work." I said.

"I'm too lazy for that." Said Serenity. We all chuckled and then finished our breakfast.

After breakfast, I went to my locker. When I opened my locker, there was a note inside all folded up. When I unfolded it, the word "ugly" was written inside of it. Then I turned around and saw Ivey and her friends laughing and pointing at me. I crumpled up the note, threw it on the floor and walked away.

Later that day was science class. When I walked into the classroom, Serenity was next to my seat.

"Oh, hey Autumn!" She said.

"Hey, Serenity. You switched seats?" I asked.

"Yep, I asked Ms. Dobbins and she said it was ok." She said.

"Cool!" I said. Ms. Dobbins walked up to us.

"Yes. But please just no chatter during my lessons. I don't go for nonsense in my class." She said.

"Don't worry. We won't!" Said Serenity. Ms. Dobbins nodded and walked away. Suddenly, I felt something hit the back of my head. I turned around and saw that it was Ivey and Zoey messing with me again. They threw a paper ball at my head.

"Do you mind?" I asked.

"Oops, sorry. I didn't see you there!" Said Ivey, sarcastically. Then they both laughed again. I should throw another one back at her, but harder. But I didn't want to start something, so I turned back around. But then, Serenity turned around.

"Why don't you just leave her alone?" She said.

"Why don't you just mind your own business?" Said Zoey.

"Why don't I take this pencil and shove it up your-?" I interrupted her.

"Dude!" I yelled. She turned back around.

"What? I was about to say nostril!" She said. I sighed in relief. Ms. Dobbins walked over to Serenity and I.

"Girls. I thought we talked about this. No nonsense in my class." She said.

"But they started it!" I said.

"It doesn't matter who started it. You're just lucky class didn't start yet. But as soon as that bell rings, no chatter and *no nonsense*." She said. Then she walked away, and the bell rang.

"Ok, class, you should be in your seats now. Today we'll just be going over what we learned yesterday. Can anyone tell me what's the charge of an electron?" Said Ms. Dobbins. Nobody raised their hands. Ms. Dobbins looked around.

"Hmmm, how about you Autumn? Can you tell me the charge of an electron?" She asked me.

"A negative charge." I said.

"That's correct." She said, writing it on the board. Zoey scoffed.

"Nerd!" She yelled out. Then the whole class laughed, while Serenity and I glared at her.

"Ok, quiet down, class." Said Ms. Dobbins. I was really confused as to why the teacher would correct Serenity and I, but wouldn't correct the kids who actually *were* in the wrong. But I guess it's ok.

"Ivey, why don't you tell me the mass of an electron?" She said. Ivey thought for a second.

"62?" She said. Serenity and I snickered at her because that answer was *way* off.

"What are you dorks laughing at? Autumn, you're 'so smart'. Why didn't you answer the question?" Yelled Ivey.

"Because she wasn't called on, Ivey. There's no need to be rude. That goes for you too, Autumn. Everyone makes mistakes." Said Ms. Dobbins.

"But can anyone answer my question?" She continued.

"Go ahead, Autumn. Tell her the answer. I'm sure you have it all figured out, right?" Said Ivey, sarcastically. Uh, oh. Somebody's *mad.* I rolled my eyes and turned around to face her.

"The estimated mass of an electron is 9.109e-31 (9.109 x 10 to the negative 31st power)." I said. Then I flipped my hair and turned back around. Serenity gave me a high five. Ivey scoffed.

"Geek." She said. Then everyone laughed again. Are you kidding me? She's actually getting mad at the fact that I knew a right answer. How petty!

"Guys, we've been over this already. No nonsense in my class. You guys wouldn't like to be sent to the principal's office, now would you?" She threatened. The four of us shook our heads no.

"Ok, then pay attention and *stop talking*." Said Ms. Dobbins. Then, finally, it was quiet for the rest of the class.

Later that day, in study hall, I was doing my homework when Tara walked up to me.

"Hi, Autumn!" She said. I looked up at her.

"Hey, Tara." I said. She looked down at my paper.

"Whatcha working on?" She asked.

"An assignment for art class. We're doing self-portraits." I said. I showed it to her.

"That is really cool! You're such a good artist." She said.

"Thanks." I said. Lauren walked over to us.

"Hey, Autumn. Hi Tara." She said.

"Hey!" We both said.

"So, guess what crazy thing Ivey did this time." I said.

"Uh oh. What now?" Asked Lauren, annoyed. I giggled.

"She called me a geek because she was mad that I got an answer right." I scoffed. Lauren and Tara both laughed.

"Oh, my gosh. That's ridiculous!" Said Lauren.

"I know right. Ivey can be so petty sometimes. Right, Autumn?" Tara asked.

"Yeah, she *can* be really petty. But on top of that, Ms. Dobbins didn't say anything to her when she called me a name, but then she got mad at Serenity and I for standing up to her." I explained.

"Really? Ms. Dobbins is usually so sweet. Everyone gets along with her." Said Tara.

"Well, for some reason she does *not* like me. I don't know why; I've never done anything wrong to her." I said.

"Just give it some time, she'll warm up to you." Said Tara. Then, the bell rang and everyone went to their next class.

That day when I got home, I walked in and my mom was in the living room.

"Hey, sweetheart! How was school today?" She asked.

"It was ok. I had some more problems today, and that teacher Ms. Dobbins seems to be a bigger problem than I thought." I said.

"Uh, oh. What happened?"

“Well first things first, Lauren and I ride the bus together so I won’t have to ride alone.”

“Well, that’s good! What else happened today?”

“Well, when I got to school today, I opened my locker and a note fell out with the word ‘ugly’ written inside of it.”

“What? Who wrote that note?”

“Probably Ivey and her friends, when I opened the note, they were standing around laughing and pointing at me.” I said, rolling my eyes.

“Just ignore them. You are far from ugly. Know why? Because you look like me, and your mom’s not ugly.” Said mom. I chuckled.

“But that’s not all that happened. Another good thing is that Ms. Dobbins let Serenity sit next to my seat, so that was good. But then, before class started Ivey and her friend threw a paper ball at the back of my head. And then when I said something to her, Ms. Dobbins came over and told us to stop talking.”

“They threw something at you?”

“Yep. But even after class started, the second time Ivey insulted me, Ms. Dobbins still didn’t say anything to her, she just kept saying stuff to me. But eventually she did when Ivey got mad because she got an answer wrong but I got it right.”

“Well those aren’t really big problems, Autumn. There are a lot of kids in the world who are having a way more difficult time in school than you. Just give it a little bit more time, I’m sure things will pick up eventually.” Explained Mom.

“Ok.” I said. After I finished talking to my mom, I went to the kitchen to start working on my homework.

Chapter 4- The Portrait

The next day, as first period was starting, I walked in and saw Jackson.

"Hey Autumn!" He said.

"Hey Jackson! What's up?" I said.

"Nothing much, you?"

"Same." I answered back. There was an awkward silence.

"So, are you excited about the winter formal coming up?" Asked Jackson. Before I could even answer back, I felt someone pull my hair really hard, causing me to fall out of my chair! I landed on the floor on my back, then I heard the class laughing. I laid there for a second, trying to figure out what had just happened. Ivey stood over me laughing.

"You alright, Autumn? You had a little tumble." She said, sarcastically. The class laughed harder. I sat up and looked around and the whole class was staring at me laughing.

"HEY! What was that for?" I asked. Eventually I realized that was a really stupid question. That's just like asking why does a snake bite. I guess Ivey was thinking the same thing, because she looked at me in confusion and laughed again with the class. Jackson stood up.

"Seriously, Ivey? What gives?!" He said to her. Ivey rolled her eyes.

"Oh, don't act like you didn't love it." She said back. Then she winked at him, then skipped away to her seat. Jackson helped me stand up.

"You okay?" He asked.

"I'm fine. But now I feel like my hair just got sucked into a vacuum cleaner." I said, rubbing my scalp. Jackson chuckled.

"Don't worry about Ivey, she's just being obnoxious." Said Jackson. Just then, the bell rang and everyone ran to their seats. The teacher walked in. Class went pretty smoothly for the rest of class. Then, the bell rang and everyone went to their next period class.

Later that day, I was on my way to science class. As I was walking through the hallway, I heard a group of people coming up behind me. Then I felt someone step on the back of my ankle. And before I could look and see who it was, someone else came and bumped me, causing me to crash into a locker. I looked and saw Ivey and her friends laughing and pointing at me.

"Oops, sorry Autumn! I didn't see you there." Said Ivey, sarcastically. Then they all laughed and ran away. I glared at them as they walked away. I scoffed at them and then walked into the classroom and sat down in my seat. When the bell rang, everyone ran to their seats. Ms. Dobbins went to the front of the classroom.

"Ok class, today we're just going to be working on these worksheets I'm about to hand out. When you're done the worksheets, you can just work on something from another class." She said.

She started handing out the worksheets and everyone got to work. The worksheets were pretty easy, so I finished within 15 minutes. So, I decided to work on my self-portrait for art class. After about 5 minutes, Serenity finished her worksheet and looked over at my portrait.

"Whatcha workin on, Autumn?" She asked.

"It's a self-portrait for art class." I said. I showed it to her.

"That's really cool! How long did this take?"

"About a week. But it's not finished yet. It's due in 2 days."

"I think you'll be getting an A!" I smiled.

"Aww, thanks!" I said. Ms. Dobbins walked over to us.

"Girls, quiet down over here. Ok?" Said Ms. Dobbins.

"Ok." I said

"Sorry, Ms. Dobbins." Said Serenity. Before Ms. Dobbins walked away, she looked at my portrait. She picked it up and held it in front of her.

"What's this supposed to be?" She asked, sort of loud. The class looked at her and laughed. I tried to take it back from her.

"Wait, it's not finished yet!" I said.

"Clearly." Said Ms. Dobbins, turning her nose up at my portrait. The class laughed again. Clearly? What's that supposed to mean? It doesn't look that bad! I just have to erase the sketch lines! Plus, *I* thought it was surprisingly good for an 8th grader.

"I told you to do work from another class. Not doodle!" Said Ms. Dobbins.

"But it's not-!" Before I could even defend myself, Ms. Dobbins TORE MY PORTRAIT IN HALF! I gasped in horror. I was crushed! I had spent so long working on that and now it's GONE!

"MS. DOBBINS!" Serenity and I both shrieked. She then continued to rip it to pieces until it was nothing more than these tiny, microscopic pieces of what used to be all my hard work!

"She wasn't doodling! That was her art project!" Yelled Serenity.

"That I've spent so long working on! And it was due in two days." I said, on the verge of tears.

"Well, now maybe you can spend the next two days *crying* about it! NO DRAWING IN CLASS!" She yelled. I was in such shock and disappointment that I couldn't even respond to her without getting upset. Serenity must've been reading my thoughts because she spoke for me. I needed to stay calm as I was in enough trouble already.

"Well, you said when we were done our worksheets to work on something from another class, and that's what she did." Said Serenity.

"Are you sassing me?" Said Ms. Dobbins. Serenity looked at her confused.

"Oh my gosh, this has got to be a joke." I said, once I was finally able to talk.

"You! I don't even want to hear your voice. And Serenity, mind your own business, this conversation doesn't concern you." Said Ms. Dobbins. I am in complete shock. What am I supposed to tell my art teacher when I don't have my project?

"Now both of you just work on something from a different class and I'd better not hear anymore nonsense from you for the rest of the class. Got it?!" Said Ms. Dobbins. Serenity and I both nodded our heads. Not because we agreed with her, but because we both wanted her to go away. Ms. Dobbins nodded and walked away.

Suddenly I heard some snickering behind me. I turned around and it was Ivey and her stupid friend Zoey laughing at me. I turned back around and put my head down on the desk. Now I have to start all over on this project, thanks to Ms. Dobbins. I felt horrible. Serenity patted my back.

"It's ok, Autumn." She whispered.

"No, it's not. I spent so long working on that project and now it's gone!" I said.

"Mehhhh, I spent so long working on that project and now it's gone!" Said Zoey, mocking me. Then her and Ivey snickered behind us again.

"Ignore them. And if you can't finish your project on time, you can always just explain what happened and ask for an extension." Said Serenity.

"Yeah, I guess you're right." I said. Serenity nodded, and the both of us started working on more homework from other classes. Suddenly, I heard some more snickering behind us.

"That kind of *was* an ugly portrait." Whispered Zoey.

"Well, it was a *self-portrait* after all." Whispered Ivey. I started to get even more annoyed.

"What if she started drawing another one and Ms. Dobbins destroyed *that* one too?" Whispered Ivey. They both snickered again.

"Oh my gosh. That would be amazing!" Whispered Zoey. Serenity leaned over.

"Ignore them, they're just trying to get you all worked up again." She whispered.

"She's not even that good of an artist, she'd probably fail anyway." Said Ivey. Suddenly I lost it and whipped my head around.

"I am *so* that good of an artist. Now back off!" I said back to them.

"For crying out loud, Autumn. Leave us alone!" Yelled Zoey.

"Yeah, we weren't even bothering you!" Yelled Ivey. Ms. Dobbins walked over to us again. Oy, here we go again.

"What's going on over here this time?" Asked Ms. Dobbins, kind of annoyed.

"Autumn won't stop bugging us!" Said Ivey.

"That's not true! They keep mumbling things about me to each other. And they called me a bad artist." I explained. Ivey gasped dramatically.

"I did no such thing!" She said, obviously lying.

"Yeah, she's probably hearing things!" Said Zoey. The class laughed at that comment.

Suddenly, I got even more mad. One, because Ms. Dobbins made fun of my portrait and then destroyed it. Two, because I have to start all over on this project. Three, because Ivey and Zoey are *still* making fun of me and four, because now *I'm* getting blamed for everything that happened. I couldn't stand to be there anymore. I jumped up out of my seat.

"Can I take a walk?" I asked, impatiently.

"NO! And sit down!" Yelled Ms. Dobbins. I sat down. But I wasn't happy about it.

"Ms. Dobbins, I-" Ms. Dobbins interrupted Serenity.

"NO! AND BE QUIET!" Yelled Ms. Dobbins, again. Serenity raised up an eyebrow at her.

"You don't even know what I was about to say." Said Serenity.

"I don't care what you have to say. I'm so sick and tired of you two always starting trouble in here. One more peep from you the rest of the class and you're going to the principal's office! Got it?!" Yelled Ms. Dobbins.

"But I didn't-!" Ms. Dobbins interrupted me again.

"I said 'got it?!'" Yelled Ms. Dobbins. Serenity and I both rolled our eyes and hung our heads down.

"Ok." We said, quietly. Ms. Dobbins walked away. Serenity and I both looked at each other in shock wondering what the heck just happened. We just eventually gave up and stayed quiet for the rest of the class. Of course, Ivey and Zoey were still snickering and mumbling stuff behind us again, but we just ignored them and did some other work for the rest of the class.

Soon, the bell rang for lunch and everyone started to get up and leave.

"Wait, Autumn! Could I speak with you?" Asked Ms. Dobbins. I looked over at Serenity and rolled my eyes, where Ms. Dobbins couldn't see me. Serenity snickered with me.

"Ok, Ms. Dobbins." I said, sitting back down. Serenity sat down with me.

"Oh, not you Serenity. I just want to speak with Autumn." Said Ms. Dobbins. Serenity and I looked confused.

"Wait, why does Autumn have to stay behind?" Asked Serenity.

"That doesn't concern you, just go to lunch." Said Ms. Dobbins. Serenity walked to the door, looked back at me and then mouthed "talk later?". I nodded and she left.

"Ok, Autumn. About today's class-" I interrupted her. I was not in the mood for anymore accusations.

"Ms. Dobbins, I just wanted to make it clear that I wasn't the only one talking. And the only reason I got so mad was because Ivey and Zoey were making fun of me behind me!" I explained.

"Autumn, this isn't about Ivey or Zoey or Serenity, this is about you and your behavior. The way you acted in my class was completely unacceptable."

My behavior is unacceptable? Look who's talking! The one who tore my portrait to pieces.

"But Ms. Dobbins, I wasn't trying to start any trouble. And you tore my portrait to pieces that was due in two days, and then told me to cry about it!"

"Watch your mouth with me, young lady! Don't you know I'm old enough to be your mother? Do *not* raise your voice at me again."

Trust me, she doesn't want to involve my mother. That wouldn't be good for anyone.

I was confused. When did I raise my voice at her? And what does her being old have to do with any of this?

"Ok, you know what? I'm tired of your mouth. You are going to sit in this seat and not say a word until I tell you to get up and leave. Got it?!" Said Ms. Dobbins.

"But this is my lunch period and-". Ms. Dobbins cut me off.

"I said 'got it?!'" She yelled at me. I paused for a second trying to figure out what had just happened. Eventually I spoke up.

"Ok." I said. But I wasn't all that happy about it. Ms. Dobbins walked back to her desk and sat down.

"Feel free to work on any other homework, but no using your phone and do not make a sound." She explained. I nodded and Ms. Dobbins pulled out some kids' tests and started grading them.

I sat there for around 15 minutes before I started getting impatient. I looked at the clock and it was 12:15. My lunch period is halfway over already! I raised my hand.

"Autumn, what did I say?" Asked Ms. Dobbins.

"It's just that my lunch period is halfway over, and I'm really hungry today." I explained.

"Oh, well maybe you should've thought about that before you disrupted my class with your nonsense. You're going to sit there until I tell you to leave!" Said Ms. Dobbins.

"But-" Ms. Dobbins interrupted me.

"No buts, don't get up until I say so."

"Ok." I said.

About five minutes passed, and lunch was about to end in now 10 minutes. I grew more and more impatient and I felt like my stomach was about to touch my back! I raised my hand again. Ms. Dobbins looked up at me, kind of annoyed.

"Autumn, we've talked about this! You can't leave until I say so!" Said Ms. Dobbins.

"Ms. Dobbins, seriously. I need my lunch break!" I begged.

"Well maybe now you've learned your lesson. You can leave when I tell you to leave!" She yelled.

I was so annoyed at her and so hungry that I was seriously considering just getting up and leaving. After about 5 more minutes, I simply decided I'd had enough and started to gather my things and leave anyway. Ms. Dobbins must've caught on to what I was doing, because as soon as she saw me putting my things away, she looked up at me.

"And don't even think about getting up and leaving, because if you do, I'm writing you up." She yelled. I decided to surprise her by showing her that I knew my rights.

"Well I'm really not supposed to be here anyway. According to our student handbooks, all students are entitled to a 30-minute lunch unless instructed otherwise by a guidance counselor, nurse, vice principal or the principal himself, and you're not either, so I'll be leaving now." I said. I started getting up to leave and Ms. Dobbins turned bright red. It was so funny, but I couldn't even bother to laugh because of how hungry I was!

"Fine then, go to lunch. See if they'll let you go to the dance." Said Ms. Dobbins, intimidatingly. I rolled my eyes and walked out the class. I didn't care whether or not I was going to the dance or not, it's not like I'm going to get a date anyway.

I walked down to the cafeteria and tried to go to the register, but the lunch lady said all lunch lines were closed! Great, thanks a lot Ms. Dobbins. Suddenly, I saw Serenity and Lauren running at me.

"Oh, my gosh. Autumn! Are you ok?" Asked Serenity.

"Where were you?" Asked Lauren.

"Ms. Dobbins kept me from going to lunch because I 'wasted time in class'." I said, mocking Ms. Dobbins.

"Yeah, Serenity told me about your portrait. I'm really sorry Autumn." Said Lauren.

"That's ok." I said.

"Wait, you're seriously saying Ms. Dobbins made you sit there the whole time and miss lunch?" Asked Serenity.

"Yeah! She would've made me wait longer, but then I reminded her of our student handbooks and what it says about lunch schedules. Then she turned bright red and let me go." I explained. Serenity and Lauren both started laughing with me. Just then, the bell rang.

"Aww DANG IT! Now what am I going to do? I can't last until 3 o clock this hungry." I yelled.

“We thought about that. So, I saved you something just in case you missed lunch.” Said Serenity. She handed me a muffin and an apple.

“Aww. Thanks a lot, you guys!” I said, taking them.

“No problem.” Said Lauren.

“By the way, you owe me $2 bucks.” Said Serenity. I chuckled, and we all headed to our next class. I ate the muffin and piece of fruit on the way to class. I was pretty much good for the rest of the day.

Chapter 5: The Smoothie

The next day, first period was Study Hall. I walked into the class and sat down to study for my American History quiz later that day. After about 15 minutes, Tara walked up to Lauren and I.

"Hey Guys, what cha up to?" She asked.

"Oh, nothing much. Just classwork." Said Lauren.

"And I'm studying for an American History quiz."

"Sounds cool." Said Tara. Neither of us were really in a talking mood, we wanted to get done our work, so we thought the conversation had ended quickly. Until this happened.

"So Autumn, what happened with you and Ivey yesterday?" She asked. Lauren and I both looked at each other, because we assumed not a lot of people would know about that.

"How did you know something happened yesterday?" I asked.

"She seemed really annoyed with you yesterday. She was going around telling everyone how petty and mean you can be. It was ridiculous." Said Tara. I was shocked. How dare she go around saying those things about me!

"What? That's not what happened at all! Remember my self-portrait that I was working on?" I said.

"Yeah, what about it?" Asked Tara.

"Well, I was working on it in science class because I was done my work and the teacher said work on something from a different class. So, I did, and when Ms. Dobbins found it, she made fun of it and then TORE IT TO PIECES!" I yelled.

"Oh, my gosh. Seriously?!"

"I know right! And then on top of it, Ivey and Zoey were instigating behind me, mumbling stuff about me, and they called me a bad artist. And then lied to Ms. Dobbins that I was bothering them."

"Wow!"

"That's not even the worst part! Then, after class, Ms. Dobbins made me stay after class for almost the whole lunch period! I didn't even get to eat lunch yesterday! I had a muffin and an apple."

"Oh, that explains why Ivey talked about you so bad yesterday!"

"What else was she saying?"

"She was talking about how you lie so much and what a bad artist you are." I started getting angry again. How dare she call me a bad artist! I'm getting really tired of her. I didn't really know what to say. But all I knew was that I had to clear up these rumors. I decided to tell Tara the real reason Ivey doesn't like me.

"None of those things are true! She's just mad because she's jealous of my friendship with Jackson."

"Wait, but I thought Jackson was dating Ivey." Said Tara.

"I know that but.... I don't know, it's skeptical." I said.

"How?"

"I feel like even though Jackson hasn't talked to me that much, he still talks to me more than he talks to Ivey, his girlfriend. And I'm sure that's why Ivey doesn't like me."

"That's weird, Ivey says that her and Jackson are like a power couple. Nobody can separate them."

"Yeah, but it doesn't really seem like that. It'd be bad if Jackson actually *did* like me while he's dating Ivey."

"Yeah, Ivey would *never* let go of that."

"I guess I do have to be careful of how much time I spend with Jackson." I said. Lauren eventually spoke up.

"Well, if you guys are friends, I don't really see what the big deal would be. Plus, if Ivey is *that* insecure about someone being friends with her boyfriend, that sounds more like a personal problem with her." She said. Lauren and I both chuckled.

"Yeah, she does seem to have a problem with insecurity. That's why I always just stay away from Jackson so I'm not on her bad list." Said Tara.

"Yeah, but Jackson and I are just friends. I don't really see what the big deal is. But I guess it's fine." I said. Then the three of us continued to work on our assignments.

At lunch, I sat down with Serenity and Lauren. Something super funny had happened the previous period and I was dying to tell them.

"You guys are *not* going to believe what happened 4th period!" I said, sitting down.

"What happened?" Asked Serenity. I tried not to laugh as I told them.

"So, right in the middle of the lesson, I was trying to write my notes, and then an eraser hit the back of Ms. Gladstone's head!-" I started laughing just trying to get the rest of the story out. Serenity and Lauren started laughing with me because of the part about the eraser.

"Oh, my gosh! Seriously?" Said Lauren, laughing.

"I'm not done yet. Then, she starts looking around for the person who threw it. And everyone was just dying laughing. And then

Robbie started laughing and bragging to Jake about how far he threw it, but he had no idea the teacher was right behind him so he-!"

Suddenly, right in the middle of my story, I felt something cold and disgusting rolling down my back. Then I realized a smoothie was being poured down my shirt! I screamed and stood up and turned around and Ivey and her friends were standing behind me, Ivey holding an empty smoothie cup.

"Oops! I really didn't mean to!" Said Ivey, sarcastically.

I ran to the bathroom and looked at myself in the mirror; I was a wreck! There was strawberry banana smoothie on me and my new white shirt was *ruined.* Soon, Serenity and Lauren came running in looking for me.

"Autumn! You ok?" Asked Lauren.

"Oh, yeah. I just love having smoothie in my clothes!" I said, sarcastically.

"It's ok, you can just-" I interrupted Serenity.

"WHY DO THEY HATE ME SO MUCH?! I literally just walked in one day and it feels like everyone hates me! Even the teachers hate me! It's not fair, what did I do?!" I broke down in tears. Serenity and Lauren both looked at each other.

"Autumn listen to me. I know what you're going through is hard, but Ivey is just jealous of you. You're smart, and you're really pretty, and kind. And let's be real, Jackson likes you." Said Serenity.

"But he can't like me! He's-" Just then, Ivey and her friends came running in the bathroom. My heart sank into my stomach. What was she about to do?

"Woah, Autumn, loving the new look!" Said Ivey, sarcastically. Then she and her friends laughed.

"Why don't you guys just admit that you're super jealous of Autumn?" Said Serenity.

"I am not jealous of that piece of trash." Said Ivey.

"Well why do you guys keep tormenting me!?" I asked.

"BECAUSE YOU'RE ANNOYING! You think you're better than everyone and you think you are somebody. And you think you can steal my man, but you can't. He doesn't even like you anyway. You're dumb, you're fat, you're ugly and a freak and he will never love you. Ever! Now stay away from Jackson, or else!" She said, getting close to my face. Then she stormed away as her friends followed. Serenity and Lauren hugged me and then helped me clean up and go back to class.

We somehow managed to get into the showers in the locker rooms and I got off all the smoothie that was rolling down my back. I was afraid that we'd have to search lost and found for a new pair of clothes, but luckily Serenity brought a spare set of clothes in case a food fight breaks out in the lunchroom. So, I was pretty much all good, but I was left with a terrible headache.

After I had straightened myself up, the bell rang and everyone went to class. I had science, so that means I had to face Ivey *again*! Serenity and I sat down in our seats and class began.

"Ok class, so today we're just going to be taking notes on our next chapter, so open up your notebooks." Said Ms. Dobbins. Everyone reached into their book bags and started getting out their notebooks. Suddenly, my headache got 10 times worse, I winced in pain. Serenity looked over at me.

"Are you okay?" She asked.

"Yeah, it's just my headache." I said.

"Are you sure?" She asked, again.

"Yeah, it's fine." I said. Ms. Dobbins started writing on the board as she talked about the lesson. I had pretty much zoned out at that point; my headache was so bad I could hardly focus. I raised my hand to go to the nurse's office.

"Yes, Autumn? You have a question?" Said Ms. Dobbins.

"Is it ok if I use the hall pass?" I asked.

"Not right now. You can't miss these notes, they're going to be on the test you know." Said Ms. Dobbins, turning back around. I couldn't even focus on the notes because of how bad my headache was!

"Are you sure you're alright?" Asked Serenity.

"No, I need painkillers." I said. I raised my hand again.

"Yes, Autumn?" Said Ms. Dobbins, sort of annoyed.

"Can I *please* use the hall pass?" I begged. Ms. Dobbins let out a sigh.

"Autumn, I've already told you, after class. Unless it's something important?" Said Ms. Dobbins.

"I just need to go to the nurse. My head hurts really bad."

"Sweetie, you're going to have to speak up a little bit."

"I said I have to go-" Ms. Dobbins interrupted me.

"You know what, if it's so important, why don't you tell everyone?"

"Why do I have to tell everyone?"

"Well, if it was worth interrupting an important lesson over, then you can tell the class why you interrupted them." I rolled my eyes and stood up at my desk.

"I said I have to go-" Ms. Dobbins interrupted me again.

"Come to the front of the class!" She yelled. I rolled my eyes again and went to the front of the class.

"I said I have to-" Ms. Dobbins interrupted me again!

"Louder." She said.

"Ok, this is ridiculous! I could've been back by now!" I said to her.

"Well, now maybe you know how it feels to be interrupted by a nuisance." Said Ms. Dobbins. Seriously? Now she's just being petty. The amount of time we wasted having this stupid conversation, I could've already been back from the nurse's office.

"You can go now." She said, again. I got up and walked to the nurse office.

The nurse's office didn't take long at all! I went, she gave me a painkiller for my headache, then I went back to class in less than five minutes. I basically wasted more time fooling around with Ms. Dobbins than I did at the nurse's office. Then, I came back to class and finished copying the notes. Eventually my headache went away after about 15 minutes. After class was over, the bell rang and everyone ran to their next period class.

Chapter 6: Rumors

The next day, as I was heading to the cafeteria, I ran into Jackson.

"Hey, Autumn!" He said.

"Hi." I said. Jackson paused.

"Um, I wanted to ask you a question, I just don't know how to say it correctly." Said Jackson. I started getting nervous, yet excited. What's he about to ask me? Just then, the bell for breakfast rang.

"Um, then I guess I'll just ask you later on. Bye Autumn!" He said, running away.

When I went to the cafeteria, I waited to see who he'd sit with. I saw him walk by Ivey and he looked at her as they all smiled at him. He looked like he was trying to escape, but Ivey grabbed his arm and said something to him. Then he yanked his arm back and quickly walked away. Sort of a rude way to talk to your girlfriend if you ask me.

I sat with Serenity and Lauren again.

"Hey, Autumn! Want my muffin? I'm not that hungry today." Said Serenity.

"No, thanks. I'm good." I said.

"Good choice. She just dropped it on the floor." Said Lauren. I looked over at Serenity in disgust.

"Snitch." Commented Serenity. We chuckled.

"Anyway, I saw you talking to Jackson, what were you guys talking about? I need to know every single detail!" Said Serenity.

"Nosy." Commented Lauren. We chuckled again.

"He said he wants to ask me a question, but he seems kind of nervous to ask me." I said.

"Uh oh, tea time! 8th grade style." Said Lauren, laughing. We all laughed with her.

"So, Autumn. How are you feeling since-?" Asked Lauren, referring to what happened yesterday. When Ivey poured a smoothie over my head.

"I'm fine emotionally now, but yesterday was pretty bad. Especially with that horrible headache I had.

"You know, let's not talk about it. It's over now, and at least you're feeling better now." Said Lauren.

"Yep. Why don't we just talk about our classes instead?" Said Serenity. Lauren and I both agreed, and we all decided to talk about stuff happening around the school. Eventually, the bell rang and everyone went to homeroom.

I went to the bathroom during first period, and when I was in my stall, I heard Ivey and her friends come in laughing and talking.

"I'm telling you; I'm going to look super cute for the school dance. Especially for Jackson!" Said Ivey.

"You're so lucky. Jackson Smith asked *you* to the Snow Ball!" Said Leah.

"I told you he wasn't going to ask Autumn. What would he see in her anyway?" Said Ivey.

"Wait, but isn't that why you didn't like Autumn? Because you think that Jackson likes her?" Asked Sandra. I snickered, but quietly so no one could hear me.

"No, you idiot! I don't like Autumn because she *thinks* Jackson likes her and he doesn't. I'm the one he asked to the dance, right? And not her!" Said Ivey, angrily.

"Well, Autumn told me that Jackson flirts with her a lot and she doesn't even think Jackson likes you at all." Said Tara.

I was shocked. I never said that! I only told her about how Jackson talks to me a lot and not to Ivey even though they're dating, and I thought that was skeptical. How dare she lie about me and twist my words around. Right at that moment, I wanted to burst out of the stall and tell her off, but I couldn't. I still wanted to hear what else they were saying about me.

"Well, then she's a liar. Jackson likes me very much, he hates Autumn. He even told me himself that he doesn't want to go with her because she's rude and obnoxious. So, she's got a lot of nerve." Said Ivey. I thought I was shocked before by what Tara said about me, but Jackson himself doesn't even like me.

"Let's get out of here. I don't feel like hearing Ms. Wheeler complain about us taking too long." Said Ivey. Then they all left the bathroom.

I felt terrible. I was so attracted to Jackson that actually thought I had a chance with him. But I can't blame Jackson. After all, they're dating. But I didn't know he said all of those things about me. And I couldn't believe that Tara has been telling everything I say about Ivey back to her. I thought she was actually cool, but I guess not. I just don't even know how to feel about all of this. I left the stall, washed my hands at the sink and then went back to class

Later that day, I was at my locker when I saw Jackson starting to walk my way, so I opened my locker and hid my face so he wouldn't stop to talk to me. Once I saw him walk away, I shut my locker and ran to the cafeteria. I sat down with Serenity and Lauren again.

"Hey Autumn!" Said Serenity.

"Hey, Girl!" Said Lauren. I chuckled.

“Hey guys!” I said.

“So, great news! They finally put that ice cream stand in the cafeteria!” Said Serenity, eagerly.

“I know! I’m so excited. Now we can get ice cream bars whenever we want!” Said Lauren.

Pretty soon, the both of them just started going on and on about how excited they are about the ice cream stand, but I wasn’t really paying attention. I just couldn’t stop thinking about what Ivey and all those girls were saying about me earlier and how Tara betrayed me and how Jackson secretly hates my guts. I peered over at his table for a minute or two. He was sitting with his best friend Troy, laughing about something. I started thinking that maybe they were talking about me, and how much the both of them hated me. Maybe he’s hated me this whole time! Maybe-

“Autumn!” Someone yelled out. I startled for a second.

“Huh?! What?!” I stuttered. I looked back over and Serenity and Lauren were both staring at me.

“Didn’t you hear me? There’s an ice cream stand in the cafeteria!” Said Serenity. I didn’t really care for ice cream at the moment.

“Oh, yeah. That’s pretty cool I guess.” I said, nonchalantly. Then I peered back over at Jackson’s table.

“What’s wrong?” Asked Lauren. I turned back around.

“Hmm?” I asked.

“You seem kind of upset about something. And you keep looking at Jackson’s table.” Said Serenity.

“Did something happen between the two of you?” Asked Lauren.

"Well, not really. But earlier I overheard Ivey and her friends talking about me in the bathroom. And you won't believe what I overheard!" I said.

"Uh oh. What happened?" Said Serenity, kind of annoyed.

"First of all, I just found out that Tara has been going back and telling everything that we say about Ivey back to her, but with a twist." I said.

"A twist?" Asked Lauren.

"Yeah, like remember when I told her that I thought it was skeptical that Jackson talks to me more than Ivey and they're dating?" I said. Lauren nodded.

"Well instead, she went back and told her that I said Jackson's always flirting with me and that I don't think Jackson likes her at all." I said.

"What?!" They both yelled.

"That isn't even close to what you said." Said Lauren.

"Yeah, but it doesn't end there. I also heard Ivey tell the rest of them that Jackson told her that he hates me because I'm rude and obnoxious." I said. They both gasped.

"How dare that jerk!" Said Serenity, angrily.

"Yeah, you're not rude *or* obnoxious." Said Lauren. Serenity started putting her hair in a ponytail.

"In fact. I think we should all have a little 'chat' with Jackson." Said Serenity, getting up from her seat. I stopped her.

"No! Don't say anything yet. He doesn't know that I know anything." I said.

"Can't I at least pound his head in?" Said Serenity.

“Not until we know if it’s true.” I said. Serenity sat back down.

“Aww, you’re no fun.” Said Serenity. I chuckled and rolled my eyes. Then the bell rang which meant lunch was over. Serenity and Lauren stopped me before I could get up to leave.

“Wait, Autumn!” Said Lauren. I turned back around.

“I just wanted to let you know, no matter how hard middle school can get, you’ve always got us.” Said Lauren. I smiled.

“Thanks, you guys.” I said. I looked over at Serenity.

“And Serenity, try not to pound Jackson’s head in when you see him.” I said.

“Ok. But no promises.” She said. We all laughed and headed to sixth period.

Chapter 7: Troy

The next day, after I got to home room, I sat down in my seat and decided to study for a little while longer until the morning announcements. The boy in front of me turned around, so I put down my book to see what was up and it was Jackson's best friend Troy.

"Hey." He said. I was a bit confused, because he's never talked to me before, but I just went along with it.

"Hey." I said.

"You're Autumn, right?" He asked. I raised up an eyebrow at him in confusion.

"Yes." I said.

"I'm Troy." He said.

"Nice to meet you!" I said. He nodded.

"You know, I've heard a lot about you." He said. My mind automatically went to Ivey and how badly she talks about me. I rolled my eyes.

"Like what?" I asked, annoyed. He chuckled.

"A close friend of mine wants to ask you to the winter formal." Said Troy. I was curious. What boy wants to ask *me* to the dance?!

"Really? Who?" I asked.

"He's always taking about how kind and beautiful and smart you are. He must really like you!" He continued. At this point, I was *really* curious. Who is this boy?!

"Who?!" I asked, again.

"Do you remember Jackson Smith?" He asked. I was shocked. So, Jackson thinks I'm beautiful? But why did Ivey say Jackson said I was rude and obnoxious. And isn't he and Ivey dating? I was so confused. I just sat there with my mouth open. He chuckled.

"I'm assuming you do." He said, laughing. Then, I started thinking that maybe Troy was just telling me a joke, to get me all excited just so Jackson could let me down. And the smiling is all the proof I need.

"You're lying." I said, straight forward.

"Why would I lie about something like that?"

"Because you're a boy. And that's what boys do."

"Wow, sexist much." He said. I rolled my eyes.

"Well, what's your answer?" He said, again.

"What?" I asked. Is he seriously still going with this joke?

"Do you want to go to the dance with Jackson?".

I didn't know whether to say yes or no. First of all, Jackson has a girlfriend. It would be wrong of me to go for someone else's boyfriend. Even if that girlfriend is as snobby and ill-mannered as Ivey. And I don't even know if this is Jackson asking or just his friend trying to set him up. Or even if this is just one big prank and they're all going to laugh in my face if I say yes. But if I say no, and Jackson really did want to go with me, it'll break his heart, then he'll *really* hate me. So, I just decided to not give him any answer.

"Before I say anything, I want to hear this from Jackson himself. To make sure you aren't just trying to pull any jokes." I said.

"Bet." He said, shrugging. Then the announcements came on.

After 1st period, I was still in the classroom getting all my things together so I could go to my next class. Soon, Jackson came up to me.

"Hey, Autumn!" He said. I looked at him.

"Oh, hey Jackson." I said.

"So, that question I needed to ask you...." He hesitated.

"Go on." I said. I was kind of worried about what he was about to say.

"So, there's this school dance coming up and-" I interrupted him before he could finish. Mostly because I was annoyed by the topic.

"Oh yeah I heard. Have fun with Ivey." I interrupted. He looked confused.

"Ivey?" He asked.

"Yeah. You asked her, right?" I asked.

"Um no, I actually was going to ask if you'd go with me." He said. I was shocked. Jackson? Going to the school dance with me?

"Wait, what?!" I said.

"Will you be my date to the winter formal?" He asked. I thought for a second. I thought Jackson hated me. And I thought Ivey was his date. What the heck is going on here? Jackson interrupted my thinking.

"Wait, who told you I was going with Ivey?" He asked.

"I overheard her talking about me in the bathroom. And she was telling her friends that you'd never ask me because you said that you hated me and I was obnoxious and rude." I told him. Jackson rolled his eyes.

"Are you kidding me? I was talking about *Ivey* being obnoxious and rude to *you.* And I never told her I hated anybody. She twisted my words around!" He said, annoyed. I was shocked. Why would she lie to her friends about that? I needed more information.

"Wait, what do you mean? You guys are dating, right?" I asked. He rolled his eyes again and let out a sigh of frustration.

"That's just a rumor that she spreads around so that no one would want to date me. I *never* dated Ivey." He said. I always knew Ivey was a mean girl, but I didn't know she was desperate. I stood there with my mouth hanging open, looking like an idiot. He tilted his head in confusion and chuckled.

"You alright?" He asked, chuckling. I snapped out of it.

"Oh yeah. I'm fine. I guess I'm just kind of shocked. That was so low!" I said. He nodded.

"The way Ivey was talking, I thought *you* were being fake." I said, hesitantly. He chuckled.

"Is that why you've been avoiding me? And why every time Serenity walks by me, she looks at me like she wants to pound my head in?" Asked Jackson. I laughed.

"Yeah, sorry about all that." I said, laughing.

"It's cool. Ivey can be pretty manipulative." He said. Jackson paused.

"Anyway, would you go to the dance with me?" He asked again, nervously.

"Ummmm...." If I said yes, Ivey would make this year even harder for me! If I said no, she wins and I'll never get the chance to get to know Jackson.

"Can I just have some time to think?" I asked. He looked a little bit bummed out.

"Yeah, sure." He said. He walked towards the door.

"See you later, Autumn." He said, walking away. I threw my bag onto my back and zoomed out of there so fast!

At lunch, I ran to the lunch table as fast as I could to meet up with Serenity and Lauren. I sat down super quick.

"GUYS, GUYS, GUYS, I HAVE BIG NEWS!" I said. They both got excited.

"What's your news?" Asked Lauren.

"You guys might want to sit down for this one." I said. We all sat down together.

"Well what is it?! The suspense is killing me!" Said Serenity. I took a deep breath.

"So today in home- room, Jackson's best friend Troy, who sits in front of me was telling me that Jackson wanted to ask me to the dance and how Jackson's always talking about how pretty and smart and fun I am. So naturally I didn't believe him because Jackson hates me but I was wrong! At the end of 1st period, Jackson asked me to the dance and told me that Ivey made all that stuff up about how they're dating and that Jackson hates me just to keep people away from Jackson! And the part where Jackson said I was rude and obnoxious, he was actually talking about Ivey and he said that he never hated anyone, so if you really think about it, the entire thing was just a big fat lie to keep people away from Jackson. And then Jackson asked me again what my answer was but I didn't know what to say because if I said yes Ivey will make me miserable all year and if I said no then she wins. So, I just told him that I needed some time to think and I need your guys' help because now I really feel like a chicken." I said, super-fast. Serenity and Lauren both looked at each other.

"Did you understand that?" Serenity asked Lauren.

"I heard something about chickens?" Said Lauren, confused. I sighed in annoyance.

"Ivey lied about Jackson thinking I'm rude and obnoxious!" I said.

"What?!" They both said.

"Yeah, Jackson said he was talking about Ivey when he said that and that he never said he hated anybody. And he asked me to the Snow Ball!" I said, happily.

"Get out of here!" They both said, again.

"Yeah, and Jackson's best friend Troy actually gave me a hint in homeroom because he said that Jackson's always talking about me to him and that he must really like me."

"Aww."

"And I don't know if I should say yes or no to Jackson."

"Say yes!"

"But if I say yes, Ivey will be mad and treat me even worse!"

"Who cares!" They said, again. They both looked at each other annoyed.

"Do you mind?" They both said, annoyed.

"Wait, what do you mean?" I asked.

"Why should you care about Ivey feelings?" Said Serenity.

"Because if she finds out Jackson asked me, she'll get even more mad at me!" I said.

"So, let her be mad. And if she *does* try to start drama, we'll be there for you." Said Lauren. Then we all hugged it out and finished our lunches.

At the end of the day, when everyone was leaving, I was at my locker getting the rest of my stuff so I could leave. Suddenly I saw Ivey charging at me

"HEY!" She yelled, pushing me and causing me to fall on the floor. I looked up at her and then started to get back up.

"How dare you push me! What the heck is your problem?!" I yelled.

"My problem is that you asked Jackson to the dance!" She yelled.

"I didn't ask Jackson. *He* asked *me*." I said.

"Well, you better have said no!" She yelled.

"You're not the boss of me!" I yelled back at her. She looked at me shocked.

"What?!" She demanded.

"Did I stutter?" I asked. She was shocked when I said that, and so was I. But I was kind of glad I said it.

"Ok, fine. Go with Jackson! Just know, you're going to be really sorry." She said, intensely. Then she stormed off. I finished up with my locker and went outside to the buses. As I was about to get on, Jackson approached me.

"Hey, Autumn." He said, confidently.

"Oh, hey!" I said, turning back around.

"So, about earlier..." He paused.

"Keep going." I said.

"Do you have your answer yet or do you still need more time?" He asked, nervously. I took a pause.

"Of course!" I said.

"Wait... Did you say yes?" He asked, surprisingly.

"Yes."

"You.... you're seriously saying yes!"

"Yes." I said, laughing.

"Great! So, the night of the dance, I can pick you up from your house and my mom will drive us to the dance?" He asked.

"Sounds like a plan!" I said.

"Awesome. See you Monday." He said.

"See you later!" I said. I got on the bus and sat down next to Lauren.

"Hey, Autumn!" She said.

"Hey." I said.

"So, what happened?" She asked.

"What do you mean?" I said, trying to play it cool.

"I just saw you talking to Jackson! What did he say? Did he say anything about the dance? What'd you say? I need to know every single detail!" She demanded.

"Ok! Ok, chill!" I said, trying to calm her down.

"WELL WHAT HAPPENED?!" She yelled, enthusiastically.

"Well, he was asking me again would I go to the winter formal with him next Friday, AND I SAID YES!" I yelled.

"NO WAY!" She yelled. We both screamed in excitement. The bus driver cocked his head around at us.

"KEEP IT DOWN BACK THERE!" He yelled. He turned back around but I could still see him glaring at us through the mirror. We both looked embarrassed.

“Sorry....” I whispered. Then he stopped looking at us and the bus started moving. Lauren and I screamed again but quieter, so the bus driver wouldn’t hear us. Just as we started to settle down, Lauren looked out the window.

“Look, it’s your bae.” She said, happily, pointing out the window. I looked out the window and I could see Jackson waving at me through the window. I smiled and waved back as the bus drove away.

That evening, I told my mom about everything that happened, including what Jackson told me about how Ivey made all that stuff up about how they’re dating, and I told her about Troy and what he said too. My mom was super excited because this is my first school dance! And I have a date! That weekend, my mom and I picked out my dress and scheduled my hair and nail appointment. I’m so excited and can’t wait for next week!

Chapter 8: Troublemaker

On Monday, after I had just finished up with my locker, I went to breakfast to meet up with Serenity and Lauren so we could catch her up on everything. I saw them and sat down with them.

"Hey Guys!" I said, happily.

"Hey, Autumn!" They both said.

"Or should I say Mrs. Smith." Said Lauren, teasingly. I slapped her on the shoulder lightly.

"Stooooppp!" I whined. Lauren and I laughed. Serenity was confused.

"Did I miss something?" She asked.

"Oh, right! We never told her!" I said.

"Told me what? WHAT HAPPENED?" She asked, anxiously.

"I SAID YES TO JACKSON!" I blurted out.

"NO WAY!" She yelled, excitedly.

"YES WAY!" I yelled back. The three of us screamed in excitement.

"Oh, my gosh! I'm so happy for you!" Said Serenity.

"Wait, do either of *you* guys have dates?" I asked.

"I'm not going. Dance class." Said Serenity.

"Me either, babysitting." Said Lauren.

"Aww..." I said. It was kind of upsetting that my best friends couldn't go to the winter formal, but they didn't really seem to care that much, so I played it off a bit.

“It’s ok. At least you got your date with Jackson!” Said Serenity. When she said that, it made me think about how really mad Ivey was going to be. I started getting nervous.

“Yeah, but here’s the thing. How are we going to handle Ivey?” I asked.

“Don’t worry about Ivey, you just have a good time with Jackson.” Said Lauren.

“Thanks, you guys!” I said.

“Come on! Hug it out!” Said Serenity. The three of us all hugged and finished our breakfast. Then the bell rang for us to go the home room.

When I got to home room, I saw Troy in front of my seat again. I sat down and then he turned around.

“Well?” He asked, as if he already knew what happened. I smiled slightly.

“You were right.” I whispered. He put his hand to his ear.

“What was that? You have to speak louder.” He said, teasingly. I laughed.

“Ok, ok! You were right! Jackson.... likes me.” I said. He smiled.

“See, I told you.” He said. I rolled my eyes jokingly.

“How come you didn’t believe me before?” He asked.

“Because.... I heard this dumb rumor that Jackson hated me and thought I was rude and obnoxious. But turns out it was just Ivey trying to stir up trouble.” I said.

“Yeah, that does seem like something Ivey would do.” He said. I nodded.

“She’s kinda hot though.” He whispered. I looked at him in shock and he laughed.

“Seriously?!” I said.

“I’m just being honest.” He said, shrugging.

“Oh, my gosh.” I said. He laughed again. Then the announcements came on and everyone stood up for the Pledge of Allegiance. After the Pledge of Allegiance, some more announcements started coming on.

“The Snow Ball Winter Formal is on Friday, December 10 from 7:00 to 11:00 in the gym, tickets are being sold in the main office or you can pay at the door at the night of the dance. Admission is $15 per person. Anyone caught dancing or wearing anything inappropriate will be removed immediately. All basketball, ice hockey and winter track tryouts will be held Monday through Thursday on the football field. Will the following students please report to the main office immediately following announcements? Emily Ross, Eric Brown, Kylie Waters, Autumn Johnson, Jordan Austin. And that’s all the announcements for today. Have a great day everyone.”

I was shocked to hear my name being called down to the office. Did I do something wrong? I was scared. I started to gather my stuff together and head down to the office. I walked down to the office and went inside. I walked up to the front desk.

“Hi. I’m Autumn Johnson, I was called down on the morning announcements?” I said to the receptionist.

“Ah yes. The principal wanted to speak to you about something. It’s the second door on your right.” She said. I went down to where she said his office was and I knocked on the door.

“Come in.” I heard him say. I walked into his office and closed the door behind me.

"Hello, Autumn. Please take a seat right over there." He said, motioning to the seat in front of him. I sat down. I got even more nervous. Did I do something wrong? Did something happen?

"So, Autumn Johnson. I'm sure you've heard about The Snow Ball coming up." He said.

"Uh, Yes." I said.

"Well, uh... you can't go." He said, bluntly. I was shocked. What did he mean I can't go to the dance?!

"What?! Why?" I asked.

"We've been receiving some complaints from teachers who say that you're a regular problem in their class and insist that you don't go. And it's a rule that if a teacher complains about a student, then that student cannot attend the Snow Ball." He said. I sat there with my mouth open. What teacher would complain about *me*? The only teacher that has a problem with me is.... of course! Ms. Dobbins! But I couldn't just go off of assumptions, I wanted to make sure.

"Which teachers?" I asked.

"I can't give you that type of information." He said. I slouched in my seat, I felt like I was about to cry. As soon as I get a date, I can't attend the dance!

"Ok, I'll tell you what. You're normally a good kid and I don't have any problems with you. So, we're going to do a small investigation to get to the bottom of this. But as of now, you are not allowed to attend the dance. Understand?" He said.

"Yes." I said.

"Ok, you can go ahead to first period now." He said. I picked up my book bag and left his office and headed to first period.

4th period was science today, which meant I had to spend *another* 45 minutes with Ms. Dobbins. But not only that, but Ivey and Zoey are there too. Oh brother. I walked into the classroom and Serenity was there.

“Hey there, Mrs. Smith.” She whispered. I bumped her.

“Stooopp.” I whined, jokingly. She laughed.

“Hey, why’d you get called down to the main office this morning?” Asked Serenity. I looked around to make sure Ms. Dobbins, Ivey and Zoey weren’t listening.

“You are not going to believe this. But I can’t go to the Snow Ball with Jackson.” I whispered. She looked shocked.

“What? Why?” She asked.

“The principal said some teacher complained about me insisting that I shouldn’t go to the dance.” I whispered back.

“Why are we whispering?” She whispered.

“Because....” I looked around again, to make sure no one was listening.

“Because I think the teacher who complained about me is Ms. Dobbins. The other day, when I left her class after she kept me during lunch, she threatened me and said, ‘See if they’ll let you go to the dance’. And she’s the only teacher who has a problem with me.” I whispered lower.

“Yep, it was definitely Ms. Dobbins. You’re not even a troublemaker!” Said Serenity. Ms. Dobbins walked over to us and my heart dropped.

“Shh!” I said to Serenity. We both got quiet.

“Hello, Serenity, Autumn. Lovely day, isn’t it?” She asked. I was kind of confused. Is she trying to start a conversation with us? We both nodded.

"So, what have you guys been up to this weekend? Any plans?" She asked, again.

"Well.... my mom and I picked out my dress for the Snow Ball already." I said.

"Hmm. Well, try not to get too excited about it. They don't accept problem students at school dances, Autumn." She said, getting closer to us. Then she smirked at us and walked away. Serenity and I were shocked that she even said that to us! That was all the proof I needed to assume that Ms. Dobbins is the one who reported me. Serenity and I looked at each other.

"Did you just see that?! Now I *know* Ms. Dobbins is the one who reported me." I said, angrily.

"Yeah!" Said Serenity. Just then, the bell rang and everyone started running to their seats.

"We'll talk at lunch." I whispered to Serenity.

"Ok, everyone. Open up your textbooks to page 75." Said Ms. Dobbins. We all opened up our textbooks and started our lesson.

Later that day, at lunch, I ran into Jackson on the way to my table.

"Hey, Autumn!" He said, happily.

"Hey, Jackson!" I said, happily.

"I can't wait for Friday. I already picked my suit." He said, smugly. I started to get sad all over again. If I couldn't go to the dance, then that means I can't go out with Jackson either! Jackson must've been reading my facial expressions because he knew something was up.

"You okay?" He asked. I got scared to tell him because I knew he'd be disappointed. But I decided to just tell him. I paused for a second.

“Come on, you can talk to me.” He said. I took a deep breath.

“Remember this morning, when I got called down to the main office?” I asked.

“Yeah, I’ve been meaning to ask. What was that all about?” He asked.

“Well.... a teacher complained about me to the Principal.... and insisted that I shouldn’t go to the school dance because I’m a ‘regular problem’.” I said, doing air quotes when I said, “regular problem”. Jackson looked shocked.

“What?! You’re not a problem!” He said.

“Exactly! The only teacher I have a problem with is Ms. Dobbins and that’s only because she’s a *jerk*!” I said, angrily. Jackson looked at me shocked. I suddenly realized how angry I probably looked and took a deep breath.

“Sorry. She’s just really rude to me all the time for no reason.” I said. Jackson chuckled.

“You’re good. It’s just that I’ve never seen you mad before.” Said Jackson. I chuckled.

“But what bothered me even more about it is that before class today, she told me not to get excited about going to the dance because ‘they don’t accept problem students at school dances’.” I said.

“That’s bogus! You’re far from a problem kid.” Said Jackson.

“Thanks!” I said. Jackson smirked.

“Anyway, hopefully I still have a chance to make it to the dance. The principal says since I’m normally a good kid, they’re going to conduct some sort of investigation to see what it is the teacher was talking about. And if I’m clear, then they’ll let me go!” I said.

"That's good. I'm sure they won't find anything. You're not a bad kid." He said. I smiled at him.

"Yeah, I hope so." I said.

"I'm going to go grab something for lunch. See you later, Autumn." Said Jackson, getting into the lunch line.

"See you later!" I said, waving. I sat down at my table.

"Hey Guys!" I said to Serenity and Lauren.

"Hey, girlie!" Said Serenity.

"Serenity told me everything that happened with Ms. Dobbins. I'm really sorry Autumn." Said Lauren.

"It's whatever." I said, playing it cool.

"I can't believe a grown woman can be so miserable to the point where she'll stop at *nothing* just to make a 13-year-old girl miserable." Said Serenity.

"Tell me about it." I said, rolling my eyes.

"But it's cool. The principal says that I'm normally such a good kid, so they're going to do some kind of investigation to see what the problem was. And if they don't find anything then I can go to the dance!" I said, smiling.

"Ok, then you're pretty much in the clear. You literally never get in trouble except in Ms. Dobbins class. And she never even has a real reason to discipline you." Said Serenity.

"I know, right! It's almost like it's her hobby to torture me." I said. The three of us laughed.

"Yeah, I think you'll be fine, Autumn." Said Lauren.

"Yeah, I sure hope so." I said.

Chapter 9: The Back of the Classroom

The next day, I went to my locker and started putting my stuff in my locker when I saw Ivey and her friends walking towards me. Here we go again. I rolled my eyes and turned towards them.

"What did I tell you?" Demanded Ivey.

"What are you talking about?" I asked.

"I told you to say no to Jackson! Leave him alone, he's *mine*." Said Ivey.

"Jackson isn't an object, he doesn't 'belong' to anyone. And anyway, I can't go." I said. Ivey and her friends looked shocked.

"What do you mean?" She asked.

"I can't go to the dance with Jackson." I said. Ivey was pretty surprised. But she still smirked at the fact that she basically wins now.

"Why? Is it because you couldn't afford a dress?" Asked Zoey. Then they all laughed. I rolled my eyes. I decided to just go ahead and tell Ivey because she was going to find out anyway.

"No, because the principal said I couldn't go." I said. I just wasn't going to tell Ivey the full reason because that will make her treat me even worse in Ms. Dobbins class. She and her friends laughed.

"Wow! Total chaos and I didn't even have to lift a finger. Karma's got you good." She snorted. Then they all flipped their hair and walked away laughing. I scoffed at them and went to the cafeteria with Serenity and Lauren.

Later that day, in science class I went to go sit in my seat and Ivey was sitting in my seat and Zoey was sitting in Serenity's. I stopped for a second and looked around to see what changed. The seating arrangements looked the same as before, except for Ivey and Zoey. Zoey cocked her head around at me.

“What are you looking at?” She asked.

“Right now, I’m wondering why you’re in my seat.” I said. Ms. Dobbins walked up.

“Hello, Autumn. I see you’ve noticed the new seating arrangements.” She said.

“Oh! You switched me and Ivey?” I asked. She chuckled.

“Oh, no! From now on Ivey and Zoey are going to be sitting in the front, and you and the rest of the troublemakers can sit in the back where you belong.” She said. I was shocked when she said that. I don’t “belong” in the back of the classroom, I’m not a problem kid! Ivey and Zoey started laughing.

“What?! I’m not a troublemaker.” I said.

“Honey, I didn’t ask you how you felt. Now go sit in the back before I call the principal down here.” She threatened. I was baffled. What is wrong with her? First, she stops me from going to the dance, and now she sits me in the back of the classroom just to humiliate me?! I stared at her in shock, with my mouth open.

“You’re in the last column third row. And close your mouth, before you catch a fly.” Said Ms. Dobbins, walking away. Ivey and Zoey laughed and pointed at me.

“Yeah, go ahead and sit in the back, troublemaker.” Said Ivey. Then they laughed again as I made my way to the back of the classroom.

Serenity was nowhere near my seat either. She got to remain in the front, across the room from where we previously sat. And I couldn’t even see the board from where I was sitting! Soon the bell rang and class started.

"Ok, class let's start. Today we're going to be reviewing for our test on Monday. So, start working on these equations and when you're done, do page 110 in your first semester workbooks." Said Ms. Dobbins.

She started writing some equations on the board, but I couldn't even see from where I was sitting. I raised my hand. Eventually, Ms. Dobbins turned around and saw my hand raised. She groaned and then slapped her forehead. Everyone turned around and looked at me.

"What is it now, Autumn?" She asked, annoyed.

"Is it ok if I move to the seat in front of me since no one is sitting there right now?" I asked. She sighed. The class laughed at her annoyance.

"No, now do your work." She said firmly. Then she turned around and started writing the equations again.

Well, *excuse me* for trying to do my work properly. I got annoyed, because one; she moved me to the back of the class knowing that I can't see from back there, two; the fact that she's getting annoyed because I'm asking her to move, three; because she has been treating me badly since the first day I arrived at school, and four; the fact that she keeps treating me differently from everyone else! Even the kids who actually *are* troublemakers. I raised my hand again. She turned around and groaned louder at me and the class laughed again.

"What is it, Autumn?!" She demanded.

"I can't see the board from back here." I said. She looked at me as if to say "Ok, and....?". The class laughed again.

"So, what do you want *me* to do about it?" She asked, arrogantly. I got even more annoyed.

"Can I move up one seat since-" She interrupted me.

“No! Now be quiet!” She said. Then the class laughed again. She turned around and started writing some more equations. I had simply just decided I’d had enough and just moved up one seat anyway, and I didn’t really care how she felt about it. Then I started copying down the equations we were supposed to solve. Eventually, she turned around again.

“Autumn! What are you doing?!” The class turned around and looked at me.

“I couldn’t see, so I moved up one.” I shrugged. Then I continued writing down the equations. Ms. Dobbins started walking to where I was sitting.

“I told you to stay where I’ve put you. You can’t even follow one simple direction?” She asked.

“Oh, don’t worry. I’ll move back when I finish copying the equations.” I said, clearly without even caring anymore at this point.

“Not ‘when I finish copying-‘ GO BACK TO YOUR SEAT!” She said, mocking me. I picked up my paper and went back to my previous seat. She walked back to where I was sitting and stared at me for a second, I stared back at her. The class was extremely quiet by this time, silently watching what would happen next.

“You know what Autumn? One day life is going to correct you and you won’t like it.... If you continue to act the way you do to me, one day you’re going to do it to the wrong person and it won’t be pretty.... You need to change the way you act because no one is going to ever like you if you don’t.... You’re nothing but a trouble making little girl.... and if you don’t figure out what it is that you need to fix about yourself and fix it, that’s all you’ll ever be.” She said, getting close to my face.

I had no words at that point. She’s a teacher! I’m a 13-year-old girl! How does she not see something wrong with the way she talks to me? You don't say things like that to people on your own level, let alone a teenage girl?! All because of a seat in a classroom? And in front of the entire class with everyone watching? Not only is that embarrassing, but it's degrading! I'll bet she didn't tell the principal *that* part, but if I even *sneezed* the wrong way, it would be a problem. I'm so sick of her. I wanted to just sit there.

The whole class, including me, stared at her in shock and horror. Ms. Dobbin stood there for a couple seconds, then walked away. Suddenly, I heard someone clapping. I looked over to see Ivey and Zoey clapping for Ms. Dobbins for what she said to me!

"Yes! Preach, Ms. Dobbins!" Said Zoey.

"It's about time someone put her back in her place." Said Ivey, glaring at me. I put my head down on the desk and covered up my head. I'm so done with this lady.

"Ok, class. Get started on the equations." Said Ms. Dobbins. I kept my head down on my desk. She's crazy if she thinks I'm going to finish her class work after that performance!

A couple minutes later, I felt my phone vibrate. I looked it and it was a picture of the board with a message from Serenity. It said "Here are the equations! And don't worry about Ms. Dobbins, she's just mad because she's miserable and ugly. LOL!" I chuckled at the message and started copying the equations from my phone and then solving them. Class was good for the rest of the class, and then the bell rang and everyone left.

Chapter 10: Change of Heart

The next day, in homeroom, the morning announcements came on and everyone stood up for the Pledge of Allegiance. After the Pledge of Allegiance, some more announcements came on.

"The Snow Ball Winter Formal Dance is on Friday, December 10 from 7:00 to 11:00 in the gym, tickets are being sold in the main office or you can pay at the door at the night of the dance. Admission is $15 per person. Anyone caught dancing inappropriately or wearing anything inappropriate or discriminatory will be removed immediately. All basketball, ice hockey and winter track tryouts are held from Monday through Thursday on the football field. Will the following students please report to the main office immediately following announcements? Maria Everson, Autumn Johnson. And that's all the announcements for today. Have a great day everyone."

I was surprised to hear my name being called on the announcements again. Then I thought back to what happened yesterday with Ms. Dobbins and I figured she probably reported me or something and ruined my chances of going to the dance! I rolled my eyes and got my stuff and started heading to the main office. Once I got to the main office, I went down the hall to the principal's office and knocked on the door.

"Come in!" He said. I opened the door and sat down in the chair in front of him.

"Hello. Autumn Johnson, correct?" He said.

"Yes." I got nervous, what did Ms. Dobbins tell him about me?

"Ok, so good news. We've just conducted our investigation and we found out you're all clear!" He said. I got excited! Yay! I can finally go to the dance! But how? What kind of investigation did they do?

"Wait, really?!" I asked, excitedly.

"Yep. I decided to have someone sit in the back of the classroom of the teacher who complained about you and that person reported back to me everything that went on in that class to see what it was they were talking about. And they saw that you really weren't causing any trouble. So, you're all clear, you can go to the dance." He said. I was shocked and excited. Despite everything Ms. Dobbins had put me through, I still get to go to the dance and now they see her for her true colors! I jumped up out of my seat.

"OH YEAH!" I yelled loud and obnoxiously. The principal stared at me. I sat back down slowly and awkwardly.

"I'm so sorry." I said, embarrassed. He chuckled.

"That's ok. You have a good time." He said.

"Thank you!" I gathered my stuff together.

"You can go ahead to first period now." He said. I stood up and walked out the door.

Later on, around lunch time, I was walking to the cafeteria when I saw Jackson. I decided to go and tell Jackson the good news. I walked up to him.

"Hey Jackson!" I said, happily. He looked over at me and smiled.

"Oh, hey Autumn!" He said.

"SOOO, I have good news." I said.

"What is it?" He asked.

"They're letting me go to the dance!".

"Wait really?! What happened?"

"So, you are *not* going to believe this. The principal said that they had someone sit in the back of the teacher's class for the last couple days to see if I really was as much of a troublemaker as they said I was. And I guess they saw that I wasn't and they said I could go to the dance!" I explained. Jackson smiled.

"I told you. You're far from a troublemaker." He said. I smiled.

"Thanks." I said. Soon the bell rang, which meant lunch is officially started.

"I'm going to the cafeteria. See you later Jackson!" I said, walking away.

"See you later!" He said. I walked into the cafeteria, got my lunch and sat down with Serenity and Lauren.

"Hey Guys!" I said.

"Hey, Autumn!" They both said.

"Hey, why did you get called down to the principal's office this morning?" Asked Serenity.

"You guys.... THEY'RE LETTING ME GO TO THE DANCE!" I yelled, excitedly. They both got excited.

"OH MY GOSH, REALLY?!" Said Serenity.

"Wait, what happened?!" Asked Lauren.

"You guys are not going to believe this! The principal said that they had someone sit in the back of the teacher's class for the last couple days to see if I really was as much of a troublemaker as they said I was. And I guess they saw that I wasn't and they said I could go to the dance!" I explained. We all squealed excitedly.

"Look at that, Autumn. Not even Ms. Dobbins could keep you from getting to that dance." Said Lauren.

"Yeah, especially after what she said to you yesterday. That's probably what showed them that *you* were the innocent one." Said Serenity.

"Yeah!" I said. Lauren looked confused.

"Wait, what did she say?" She asked.

"Oh, right! We didn't tell her yet." Said Serenity. Lauren looked confused.

"She gave me this ridiculously long speech on life's going to correct me and no one's ever going to like me and I'm a troublemaker and all this crazy stuff." I said. Lauren looked shocked.

"I know right! I heard the whole thing." Said Serenity.

"What is wrong with her? She's almost 30 years old and she said that to a teenager?!" She demanded.

"Exactly! So, I guess when whoever observed our class saw that they realized I'm not so bad after all!" I said, happily.

"I'd say this is a good time for a 'cheers'!" Said Serenity, holding up her drink. Lauren and I did the same thing and we clinked our drinks together.

"Cheers!" We all said. After all of that, we just talked about some more stuff that happened around the school, so it wasn't really important. After a while, the bell rang and we all went to class.

Later that day was science, and I was already dreading it because I just knew Ms. Dobbins is dying to start some trouble. I walked into the class and sat down in my seat in the back. Ms. Dobbins started walking in my direction. Oh boy, let's get this over with.

"Good afternoon, Autumn!" She said, smiling. I was confused. Why is she acting so nice all of a sudden?

"Good afternoon!" I said.

"I just wanted to let you know that I've switched your seat again with someone else again, so that you could see the board. You're going to be in the second row in the second column." She said. I was kind of glad that she moved my seat again, but I was confused as to why she was acting so sweet all of a sudden. I have a strange feeling that this is just the calm before the storm. But I just went with it for now.

"Thanks, Ms. Dobbins." I said. She walked away. I gathered my stuff and started walking to my new seat. Soon the bell rang.

Class went pretty smoothly today because Ms. Dobbins didn't have any rude remarks. I guess they finally confronted her about the way she's been treating me. After class was over, the bell rang and everyone started walking to their next period class. I was gathering my stuff when Ms. Dobbins walked over to me.

"Hold on a second, Autumn. I just wanted to have a little chat with you." She said. Well, here we go again....

"Yes, Ms. Dobbins?" I said, sitting back down.

"I just wanted to apologize for what I said to you yesterday. I realize that comment wasn't something to be said in front of the whole class like that." She said. I was sort of shocked. Ms. Dobbins, Apologizing? Was there an insult in there that I missed?

"That's okay, Ms. Dobbins." I said.

"I don't mean to be rude to you, Autumn. But sometimes it really bugs me when you don't follow directions, or trade insults with other students while I'm teaching a class. You understand right?" She explained. I understood, but it wasn't entirely true. If I'm *trading* insults with people, it means that I'm not the only person. Ivey should be punished sometimes just like me.

"I understand. But *I* just don't like it when you single me out or say something to me in front of the entire class. I feel like that's why people keep bothering me. For some reason, they get joy out of my misery!" I explained.

"Well, then. Now that we both understand each other, maybe things can be better in my class. From now on, you can just let me know when another student is causing problems with you and I will handle it. Ok?" She said.

"Ok, thanks, Ms. Dobbins!" I said, as I was getting my stuff together. I stood up and began to walk out the door.

"Autumn, Wait!" I heard Ms. Dobbins call out. I turned around. Ms. Dobbins smiled at me.

"Have fun at the dance on Friday." She said. I smiled back.

"Thanks, Ms. Dobbins." I said. To be honest I never expected to have that conversation with Ms. Dobbins. I thought this was going to be another opportunity for her to break me down. But I guess now I won't have to worry about Ms. Dobbins giving me problems! I walked out of the door and started walking to my next period class.

The next day, first period was Study Hall. I was doing work from another class when Tara walked up to me.

"Hey Autumn!" She said. I wasn't really happy to see her, especially after I found out she had been instigating problems with Ivey and I. I looked at her.

"Hey." I said. I continued to work on my assignments. Lauren didn't even bother to look at her.

"What's up with you guys?" She asked.

"Huh?" I asked.

"You guys haven't been talking to me in a while. Is everything ok?" She asked.

"Just classwork. You know." I said, curtly. I figured she'd eventually give up and turn back around.

"Yeah, classwork is pretty hard." She said. There was an awkward silence.

"So, I heard you're going to the dance with Jackson Smith! Congratulations!" She said. I smiled back at her.

"But I'd just be careful around him if I were you." Said Tara. Lauren and I both looked at each other, we both knew she was about to start her lying again.

"Why?" Asked Lauren.

"I heard this rumor that Jackson secretly hates you and thinks you're rude and obnoxious. Isn't that crazy?" Said Tara. Lauren and I both looked at each other and smirked. We both wanted to see how far she'd go with this lie, so we played along.

"Oh, no! Why would he say that?" I asked, sarcastically. Lauren snickered, so I nudged her under the table.

"Well, I heard Ivey saying in the bathroom that she thinks you flirt with him a lot and that's why he pays more attention to you than her. And it looks like Jackson doesn't like her at all. And the only reason he broke up with Ivey and asked you to the dance instead was so you'd leave him alone." She said.

Suddenly, Lauren and I just both lost our cool and just started laughing hysterically. That's almost exactly what she told Ivey that *I* said about *her*. In other words, she's busted! Tara looked confused.

"What's so funny? Didn't you guys hear me?" Asked Tara.

“Oh, we heard you alright.” Said Lauren, laughing. We both started laughing again.

“Why is that so funny?” Asked Tara.

“We already know you’re lying!” Said Lauren.

“Wait, what do you mean?” She asked, nervously.

“I was in the bathroom that time when you were telling Ivey that I don’t think Jackson likes her.” I said. Tara paused.

“Well, I’m technically not wrong. And you *do* think that.” Said Tara.

“I told you I thought it was skeptical that Jackson talks to me more than Ivey! Not that I think Jackson likes me more than her.” I said. Tara paused.

“Well- um.” She stuttered. I guess she was out of excuses.

“Just admit it. You’ve been instigating problems between the two of them just to cause more drama.” Said Lauren. Tara didn’t say anything.

“Well, I’m waiting.” I said.

“So, what if I was?” Asked Tara.

“Why would you do that?” I asked.

“Look, I don’t have time to be interviewed. I have classwork to do.” Said Tara, turning back around.

“Uh oh. Somebody’s feeling guilty!” Mumbled Lauren. We both laughed. Tara turned back around.

“Ok, you know what? I tried to be nice to you but I’m so sick and tired of you. You’re so annoying and you walk through the school like your butt doesn’t stink. And everyone here agrees with me. Ask anybody!” Said Tara. I was sort of shocked. I kind of knew that Tara was going to be upset with me about exposing her, but I didn't think she'd go and say something mean like that.

"Don't listen to her, Autumn. She's just mad because she got caught." Said Lauren.

"It doesn't matter what she says about me. We all know she lies." I said.

"Fine. Then maybe I should stop trying to be nice and I should start treating you like the piece of trash you really are. Have a nice life, Autumn." Said Tara, turning back around. Lauren and I both looked at each other.

That was crazy! I knew Tara was fake, but I didn't know she actually hated me on the down low. I'm so glad I was in the bathroom that day and heard everything because I would've fell into all of the lies that she told and I probably wouldn't want to go to the dance with Jackson.

"Don't worry about her. At least we found out she was fake before it turned into something bigger." Said Lauren.

"Yep." I said. Then, the bell rang and everyone ran to their next period class.

Nothing else really happened today, everything seemed to go by smoothly other than that.

Chapter 11: The Lunch Table

On Friday, the night of the dance, I was on my way to the cafeteria for lunch, when I saw Ivey and Jackson at Jackson's locker and it looked like they were arguing about something. I didn't want to get involved in anything, so I stood and watched from my locker. I didn't know who said what but eventually I saw Jackson roll his eyes, slam his locker shut and then walk away. Ivey looked over at me, so I tried to pretend I didn't see what was going on. She walked over to me.

"What are you looking at?" She said.

"What do you mean?" I said back.

"I just saw you looking at me, so don't look at me! Got it?!" She said. I rolled my eyes.

"Hmph. Well I see you're still going to the dance with Jackson even after I *specifically* told you he was *mine*." She said.

"Jackson told me you guys aren't even dating. You can't just tell him who he can and can't date! You're not his mother!" I yelled.

"I am giving you one last chance. Break your date with Jackson." She said, getting close to my face.

"KISS MY ELBOW!" I yelled at her angrily. She backed away from me.

"Ok, fine. Go with Jackson but you're going to be sorry. And, before you ask, no that's not a threat. That's a promise." She said, intensely. I got a little nervous for a second, so I didn't respond. Then she walked away giggling. I finished up at my locker and walked back to the cafeteria. As I was heading inside, I saw Jackson in the lunch line. I went up to him.

"Hey, Jackson!" I said. He turned around.

"Oh, hey Autumn! You ready for the dance?" He asked, awkwardly. He didn't seem focused. He was looking around as if he was looking for someone. I looked around too as if to mock him. He chuckled.

"Sorry. I just feel awkward." Said Jackson. I got nervous.

"Awkward? About what?" I asked, nervously.

"It's nothing about you. It's about Ivey. She's been acting super jealous lately because I asked you to the dance and not her." He said. He took a pause and exhaled nervously.

"We just got into a super-heated fight back at my locker. She was trying to tell me how her and I are so 'destined' to be together and that you're just 'getting in the way'. It was ridiculous." He said.

"I'm not surprised. Ivey has never liked me since the day I arrived here. I never really understood why." I said.

"Don't worry about her, she's just jealous of you. I'm not going to let her ruin our night. Ok?" He said.

"Ok!" We both smiled at each other for a while.

"COME ON! MOVE IT OR LOSE IT!" Yelled one of the kids in back of us. We both looked and realized the line had moved and we were still standing there. We both laughed and went up to the register to pay for our food. When we were done, we started walking to our lunch tables.

"So, Jackson, quick question." I said.

"Sure, what is it?" He asked.

"Is what Troy said you were saying about me true?" I asked. Jackson paused.

"What did he say?"

"He told me that you're always talking about how smart and funny and pretty I am. But I didn't want to believe him at first." Jackson did a face palm.

"Come on, he wasn't supposed to tell you about it." He said. I laughed.

"So, it's true?" I asked. Jackson paused.

"Yeah. Sorry if it sounds kind of cheesy." He said. I laughed again.

"It's not cheesy. It's adorable!" I said, smiling. Jackson smiled.

"You know, I don't think we've ever sat at lunch together." He said, obviously just trying to change the subject. But I just went along with it. I could tell our previous conversation was making him a little uncomfortable.

"How about we do that right now? And I can get Serenity and Lauren and you can get Troy and we could sit together!" I said.

"Sounds like a plan! I'll be right back." He said. He started heading over to his table to talk to Troy, so I started heading to my table.

"Hey Guys!" I said, happily.

"Hey there, Mrs. Smith!" Said Serenity. I bumped her arm playfully.

"Stoooopppp!" I said, playfully. The three of us laughed.

"So, Guys. How would you feel if for the first time, Jackson and Troy sat with us? That way we could all bond and you guys could finally meet Troy!" I said, excitedly.

"Ooh! That's sounds pretty fun!" Said Lauren. We saw Jackson and Troy coming towards our table.

"Trust me, it will be!" I said. Jackson sat next to me and Troy sat next to Lauren.

"Hey Guys!" Said Serenity.

"Hey!" Said Lauren.

"Hey!" Said Jackson.

"Sup!" Said Troy. We all just joked and laughed about stuff most of the time. At least 15 minutes had passed when I saw Troy, Lauren and Serenity look behind us with a worried look on their faces.

"What's wrong?" I asked.

"Don't look now, but Ivey and her friends are looking over here." Said Serenity. I dropped my spoon on the floor, purposely, so when I bent over to grab it, I could turn and look at Ivey's table. I looked and every single person at the table was giving us the death stare. I sat back up and looked at Jackson.

"Yep. They look like they're about to beat us up or something." I said, jokingly. We laughed.

"She's probably really mad now, especially after that argument we just had." Said Jackson.

"What argument?" Asked Lauren.

"She stopped me at my locker and was trying to convince me to break my date with Autumn. She's super jealous because I didn't ask her to the dance." Said Jackson.

"Oh, gosh." Commented Serenity.

"I guess if Troy were going to the dance, he could just ask her to get her off my back." I Said. Jackson and I both laughed.

"Hey, that was our secret!" Said Troy.

"She was joking." Said Jackson. Wait, does Jackson not know about Troy's little crush on Ivey? Whoops! Troy and I looked at each other nervously.

"Wait, you seriously like Ivey?" Asked Jackson. Troy paused nervously.

"Ok, let's be honest. She's kinda hot!" Said Troy. We laughed together.

"But seriously. Why *didn't* you ask Ivey to the dance?" Asked Lauren.

"I did! And she said yes. Well, at first. It turns out she was just trying to make Jackson jealous. But then Autumn arrived and Jackson started liking her. So, when she saw it didn't work, she broke her date with me and started trying to get with Jackson again." Said Troy, awkwardly.

"Aww, I'm sorry Troy." I said.

"It's fine. I started not even wanted to go anyway. Getting ready for that dance was too much work." Said Troy, jokingly. The rest of us laughed. The conversation started getting a little awkward, so we changed the subject. We all just started talking about our classes, goofing off and laughing about the most random things. I really enjoyed it. Then, the bell rang and everyone went to class.

Jackson walked up to me while I was walking out of the cafeteria.

"I'll see you at 7." He said, smiling. I smiled back at him.

"See you then!" I said. We both walked off to our next class.

Chapter 12: Getting Ready

Later that day, Mom was helping me get ready for the dance. I wore a baby blue dress that was strapless, glittery at the front and had ruffles at the end. Then I had on my favorite pair of silver slingback heals with glitter on them with some silver jewelry. And I decided to wear my hair with big curls at the ends, and I even wore a little bit of makeup, which I don't normally do. I just had to put the finishing touches on my look. I was in the living room while my Mom was helping me fix my dress.

"I can't believe my baby is going to her first school dance with a date!" Said Mom, happily. I rolled my eyes.

"Mom, don't start." I said.

"I'm sorry, I just can't believe it. It feels like only yesterday I was holding your bottle for you. And now you're going off on your first date!" She said, tearing up.

"This cannot be any more embarrassing!" I said. Then, my dad walked in.

"Alright, now where is this 'date' of yours?" He asked me.

"He should be here at any minute. And please don't go insane on him when you see him." I said.

"Oh, I won't. Just remember whatever he's going to do to you, I'm going to do to him." Said Dad.

"What if he kisses me?" I asked, sarcastically.

"Once again, whatever he does to you-" Mom interrupted him.

"Babe, I think she gets it." She said. Nikki and Jade, my little sisters ran downstairs.

"I want to meet Autumn's boyfriend!" Said Nikki.

"Me too!" Said Jade.

"Guys, he's not my boyfriend. And *you* two had better not embarrass me either." I said.

"And you two had better not embarrass me either!" Said Nikki, mocking me.

"Mom!" I said. Nikki laughed.

"Nikki, leave your sister alone." Said Mom.

"She started it." Said Nikki. I rolled my eyes. Just then, the doorbell rang. I stood up.

"I'll get it!" I said. My Dad stood up in front of me.

"*I'll* get it." He said. I sat back down. He opened the door and it was Jackson and his mom.

"Hello. You must be Jackson." Said my Dad.

"Yes, sir. My name is Jackson Smith." He said, holding his hand out for a handshake. My dad shook his hand.

"Come on in." Said Dad. They both walked in. Jackson looked so handsome, he had on a black suit and a baby blue tie that matched my dress. He looked GOOD! WOW!

"Hey!" I said, standing up. He looked at me, admiring my outfit.

"Hey." He said, smiling at me. My mom and dad walked over to Jackson.

"I'm Michelle, Autumn's mother." Said my Mom, shaking his hand.

"I'm Robert, Autumn's father." Said my Dad.

"It's nice to meet you." Said Jackson. Jackson's mom walked up to me.

"Hi Sweetie! My name is Jaclyn, I'm Jackson's mother." She said, holding out her hand for a handshake.

"Nice to meet you, too!" I said, shaking her hand.

"Autumn and Jackson sitting in a tree K-I-S-S-!" I ran and covered up Nikki's mouth before she could say anything else. I chuckled nervously.

"Ignore her, she's loony." I said. Jackson chuckled. Mom picked up Summer from the couch she was laying down on.

"Jackson, these are her sisters, Nikki, Jade and this is Summer, her baby sister." Said Mom, motioning to each of them.

"It's nice to meet you." Said Jackson. I uncovered Nikki's mouth.

"I'm not loony!" Said Nikki. Jackson chuckled again.

"Oh! We should get going. It's almost 7:30." I said.

"Ok, then I'll see you guys at 11:30." Said Mom.

"It was nice meeting you!" Said Jaclyn.

"Same to you!" Said Mom. My Dad came and stood next to me.

"I think he's alright." He whispered to me.

"He's great!" I whispered back.

"See you later!" I said, waving to everyone. Jackson, his mom and I walked out the door.

"So, you guys ready?" She asked.

"Yes." We both answered. We all got in the car and she drove us to the dance.

His mom stopped the car about half a block away from the school.

"Do you guys want to get out here, or do you want me to drive further up?" She asked.

"Here's fine. I want to make a grand entrance." Said Jackson. I blushed at him. Jackson's mom started tearing up.

"Mom, what's wrong?" He asked.

"It's just that my baby boy is growing up." She said.

"Oh, come on. Don't start Mom. Not now!" He said. She ignored him.

"I remember when you were just a little pea in a pod. You had those rosy cheeks when you smiled." She said, tearing up more. Jackson started getting irritated, it was kind of funny, but I didn't laugh.

"Mom!" He whined at her.

"I still have those pictures of you in your first bath!" She said. Jackson turned red from embarrassment. His mom looked at me.

"I have them right now if you want to see them!" She said to me. I put my hand over my mouth and tried not to laugh.

"Mom! Stop!" He yelled.

"Ok, ok. I'm sorry. I'll let you guys out." She said, wiping her tears. She unlocked the door and we got out.

"Thanks, Mom." He said.

"Thanks, Mrs. Smith." I said.

"Have fun! And please, call me Jackie." She said. Jackson's mom rolled up the window and drove off.

"Sorry about my mom. She just can be really over the top." Said Jackson. I suddenly lost it and just bust out laughing.

"What?" He asked.

"The bathtub!" I yelled laughing.

"Hey!"

"Sorry, it took everything I had to not laugh!"

“Ah, geez.

“It’s ok. I know how embarrassing parents can be.”

“Yeah, they really are.” Said Jackson. The both of us just started ranting on for the past half block about how embarrassing our parents are.

Chapter 13: The Dance

We finally arrived at the dance and we were still talking.

"Are you serious?!" I said.

"Yeah, she literally ran down from the bleachers and started kissing my face in front of the entire team!" Said Jackson. We both laughed. I looked over and saw Ivey and Leah sitting down at a table talking and laughing.

"Oh, no!" I said.

"What's wrong?" Asked Jackson. I pointed to where Ivey was sitting. He looked at her and then looked back at me.

"Let's not let her spoil our fun. Ok?" He said.

"Yeah, good point." I said. Suddenly the song changed and my favorite song was playing. We both gasped.

"I LOVE THIS SONG!" We both yelled, at the same time. We both looked at each other and laughed. We ran into the crowd and danced the night away!

We danced for hours, we had so much fun. I almost forgot Ivey was even there. Then a slow song came on and Jackson grabbed my hand.

"Shall we?" He asked. We both smiled. I grabbed his hand.

"We shall." I said.

As we danced to the slow song, he stared into my eyes and I stared into his. It felt like I was being hypnotized all over again, just like when we first made eye contact! It was amazing.

Soon, the regular upbeat music started playing and everyone started dancing again, except for us. We still stayed like we were while everyone danced around us. It was like we were stuck like that. Jackson stroke my hair.

"You look beautiful tonight." He said.

"You have the prettiest eyes!" I blurted out. I have no idea why I said that, but I was kind of glad I did.

He started to lean in and so did I. We were nose to nose, about to kiss. But then I started to feel scared. I was about to have my first kiss, with Jackson Smith, but suddenly I wasn't really sure if I wanted to have my first kiss yet, I don't know why. I stopped him and then backed away.

"What's wrong?" He asked.

"Sorry, it's just that I haven't had my first kiss yet, and I don't wanna rush into things. I hope you're not mad." I said.

"Why would I be mad? If you're not ready, then you're not ready. I'll wait." He said. I was actually really shocked when he said that, but I was glad he said it. I sighed.

"Thanks." I said

"No problem." He said.

"I think I'm going to go get some punch." I said. I really didn't want any punch at all, but I just needed to take a walk and think about everything that just happened. I started walking to the punch bowl when suddenly-

I tripped and fell, landing FACE FIRST INTO THE DESSERT TABLE CAUSING THE WHOLE THING TO COLLAPSE! I heard two girls laughing. Those voices sounded oddly familiar, so familiar that I started getting scared. As I was getting up, with cake and chocolate all over me and in my hair, I saw two girls standing there with their phones out, like they were recording me! As I brushed the cake out of my face, I realized it was Ivey and her best friend Leah! One of them *tripped* me to make me fall! I looked around, almost wishing I hadn't. Nearly everyone at the dance was there with their phones out doing the same thing, pointing and laughing at me! I stood there frozen; I was a wreck! Ivey walked up to me, turned me around, and put her phone in my face.

"I told you you'd be sorry, and I never break my promises!" She whispered to me. Then she pushed me causing me to fall again. Everyone laughed even harder! I panicked and ran out of the gym. I am really getting fed up with these kids. I feel like I'm going to snap; I can only take but so much. I really wished Serenity and Lauren were here right now.

I ran into the bathroom and looked at myself in the mirror. I was a mess! There was cake and frosting all over me, my dress was ruined and there were tears going down my face! Then I started having flashbacks of when Ivey poured a smoothie on my head and I was in the same position! Only this time, the mess was bigger and Serenity and Lauren weren't there to help me. All I could do was cry all over again. I decided to just call my dad to come pick me up since my night was pretty much ruined anyway.

"Hello, Dad?" I said, crying. He was immediately suspicious when he heard my voice.

"What's wrong, what happened? Did that jerk Jackson do something to you?!" He demanded. I had almost forgotten all about Jackson, but I didn't care.

"No! It wasn't Jackson, it-" I didn't want to bring it up again, so I tried to just play it off.

"Can you please just come get me?" I asked.

"Ok, I'll be there in about five minutes." He said.

"Thanks, Dad." I said.

I hung up the phone and slouched down onto the wall and cried. I figured in the meantime, I can just try my best to clean up what I could. I grabbed some paper towels and tried to get the cake out of my hair and then wiped my face with a makeup wipe. Then I started heading outside so my dad could pick me up. I was on my way down the hall when I heard a familiar voice.

"Hey, Autumn." They said. The sound of the voice so suddenly startled me. I turned around to see who it was. It was Jackson. He was one of the last people that I wanted to see me, especially after Ivey humiliated me in front of the entire school!

"Hey." I said.

"That was pretty messed up, what Ivey did to you." He said.

"Yeah." I said. I was so embarrassed I could barely even talk! I felt my phone buzz. It was my dad letting me know he was outside.

"I just wanted to say-" I interrupted Jackson before he could even finish his sentence.

"Jackson, I have to go." I said, starting to run down the hall to the side door.

"Wait, Autumn!" He said. I ignored him and left the school, got in my dad's car and he drove off. I didn't even bother to look back, all I wanted to do was go home.

Later that day, my mom was helping me clean up, since there was cake frosting and teary mascara all over my face.

"Autumn, I'm so sorry this happened to you, baby." Said mom. I shrugged.

"Why didn't you just tell me you were being bullied? I would've handled it." She asked.

I didn't think it would escalate this high. Plus, I don't need my 'mommy' to hold my hand every step of the way, I'm not a little kid." I said.

“Yes, I know you’re not a little kid, but you need to tell me when things like that happens. You can always come and talk to me.” She said. I smiled.

“Thanks, Mom.” I decided to just open up and tell her everything that had been going on.

“The truth is.... this actually has been going on for a while now. I just haven’t been talking to you about it that much because I didn’t want you to freak out.” I said.

“Autumn, baby, you don’t have to hide things from me. If you didn’t want me to overreact, all you had to do was just tell me not to.” She said.

“That’s what all moms say, but let’s face it, you guys are crazy sometimes.” I said. My mom chuckled.

“Yeah, I can admit, moms can be a little crazy sometimes. But it’s only because we love our kids and we just want what’s best for them.” She said. Suddenly, there was a loud knock at the door.

“MOMMY!” Yelled Jade. Mom ran to the door.

“What is it, Jade?” Mom asked, worried.

“I have to go potty!” She yelled. I rolled my eyes.

“Jade, you made us think there was an emergency!” Said mom.

“It *is* an emergency!” She yelled, again. Mom chuckled.

“Honey, I’m still busy with your sister right now. Go use Mommy’s bathroom, ok?” Said Mom.

“Ok!” Said Jade, skipping away. Mom closes the door and sat back down next to me. She looked back at me and gasped.

“Now there’s that beautiful smile!” She said. We both chuckled.

“So, as I was saying, you don’t have to be afraid to tell me things, Autumn. You can always come to talk me about anything. Ok?” Said Mom.

“Ok.” I said. Mom reached her arms and we both hugged each other tight.

“Now, why don’t you go take a shower, get all that stuff out of your hair.” Said Mom.

“Ok.” I said, as mom got up to walk out. She opened the door, and then looked back before she left.

“Let me know if you need anything, ok?” She said.

“Ok, thanks mom!” I said.

“No problem, sweetie.” She said. She walked out the bathroom and closed the door. Then I took a shower and washed my hair to get all the stuff that was in my hair out. It took around an hour, then I went back to my room and just laid there for the rest of the evening.

Chapter 14: Social Media

The next morning, I woke up with a terrible headache. I laid there for a while and tried to recount everything that happened at the dance last night, and to be honest I almost wished I hadn't. All the memories of everything that happened yesterday started rushing back, from the fight with Jackson and Ivey at Jackson's locker earlier Friday, all the way to me leaving the dance in a hurry. I guess Ivey was right, I was sorry that I didn't just break my date with Jackson.

I sat up in my bed and looked at the time on my phone. It was 12:00 noon! I also had multiple missed calls and text messages. From Jackson, I had a missed call, a voicemail and three text messages.

"Autumn, we need to talk."-11:28pm, Friday

"Hey, are you up??"-9:49am

"Call me when you get a chance."-10:01am

The voicemail said:

"Hey, Autumn. This is Jackson. I have something important to talk to you about. It's about what happened at the dance. Call me when you get this message. Bye."

I felt like crying again after I heard it. I didn't even stop to think about how Jackson felt after I had left him at the dance. I was just so humiliated I wanted to leave. I wanted to call him back when I heard it, but I decided to wait until I felt the time was right. I looked at all the other messages.

I had one text message from Troy that said:

"Yoooo I just heard! That was messed up. Hope all is well."-11:32am

I laughed and looked at some more messages. I had 2 missed FaceTime calls and 5 text messages from Serenity! The text messages said:

"AUTUMN"- 10:38am

"ARE YOU OK?!" -10:38am

"ANSWER THE PHONE" -10:40am

"ITS ABOUT IVEY PICK UP" -10:41am

"When you wake up, call me backkkk"- 10:43am

I did *not* feel like talking about Ivey right now, so I scrolled past it for now. From Lauren, I had a missed call and a voicemail that said:

"Hey Autumn, I just heard what happened. I'm so sorry I wasn't there to help you. And I just finished talking to Jackson and Serenity, they both really need you to call them. It sounds urgent. Hope all is well, call me back when you get this message. Buh-bye!"

I smiled because it was nice to see my friends' reaching out to me. But I couldn't bother to respond to anybody yet. I still wasn't ready to relive what happened by talking about it to more people. I can always talk to them later on.

I scrolled some more and I saw one more text message from Nikki that said:

"I'm boredddd. Will you play with me????" -10:29am. I rolled my eyes.

In the meantime, I decided to just get myself together by carrying on with my regular day. I brushed my teeth, did my hair and got dressed, and just hoped to forget everything that happened at the dance. After I was dressed, I went downstairs. Nikki and

Jade were downstairs playing dolls, Summer was in her bouncing chair watching a movie with my parents. Everyone looked at me.

"Good afternoon, sleepy head!" Said my mom.

"It's about time!" Said Nikki. My mom nudged her arm.

"Ow, what?" Asked Nikki. I started laughing.

"Hey Mom." I said. I gave everyone a hug.

"If you're hungry, I think there's some chocolate chip pancakes left over from earlier." Said Mom.

"No thanks, I'm not hungry." I said.

"Ok, then come watch this movie with us. It's pretty good so far!" Said Dad. I sat down and started watching the movie with my parents.

The movie was about two hours long, and it *was* a good movie. By the time, the movie was over, I was really hungry, so I went to get something to eat. After I was done, I came back into the living room and Nikki, Jade and Summer were holding their coats and waiting for me.

"Finally! She's back!" Yelled Nikki. I rolled my eyes again. My mom walked towards me.

"Autumn, it's such a nice and sunny day outside, so I figured maybe we could go to the outdoor ice-skating rink!" She said. I smiled, because she was obviously trying to find something to cheer me up since last night.

"And then maybe later, we could bake a cake or something!" She said again. Right when she said "cake", it reminded me of when I was at the dance, completely covered in cake in front of everyone. Mom paused, realizing how sad I must've looked.

“Oh, right. Sorry sweetie. How do chocolate chip cookies sound then?” She asked. There were cookies on the dessert table yesterday as well, but cookies sounded slightly less bad then baking a cake.

“Ok, sure.” I said.

“YAY! I LOVE COOKIES!” Yelled Nikki, excitedly.

”Yeah, me too!” Yelled Jade.

“Then I guess it’s settled, cookies it is!” Said mom.

“Yay!” Nikki and Jade yelled.

“Now Autumn, why don’t you go grab a coat so we can head out.” Said mom.

“Ok, I’ll be right back.” I said.

I ran upstairs and went in my room to find my coat. I decided to wear my red and white coat since Christmas is coming up soon. I put it on and started to head back downstairs. I checked my phone before I left and saw even more messages from my friends. I decided to ignore them and just go downstairs to my sisters. I wasn’t really in the mood to talk about the dance anymore. I went back downstairs and we got in the car and drove to the ice-skating rink.

The car ride was about 15 minutes, and we finally arrived. Once we passed through admissions, Nikki and I put on our skates and started heading onto the skate rink. Mom had to help Jade put hers on. First, we decided to just try to skate around, but we kept falling down. Once Jade got on the ice, she was a bit scared at first, so Nikki and I held her hands so she wouldn’t fall. Everything was going fine until Nikki lost her balance and all three of us fell. Nikki and I thought it was funny, but Jade started crying and saying she hurt her knee, so she got off. After a while, Nikki and I got the hang of it, so we decided to skate around for a little bit. Eventually,

Jade came back and we decided to do a train. I led, then Nikki was next, then Jade and we just skated around like that. Then I fell again and Nikki and Jade both fell on me. Nikki and I laughed it off, but Jade got mad again and got off. Soon, we started getting cold, so we headed over to the hot cocoa bar. It was amazing! We also got some soft pretzels while we were there. Once we were finished, we kept on skating and then after a while, it was time to leave.

When we got home, we took off our coats, bathed and then started getting ready for dinner.

After dinner, we decided to make the chocolate chip cookies. We got out all of the ingredients and got started. Once we mixed all of the ingredients in, we started spreading the dough onto the cookie sheet. Then, we put the cookies in the oven.

"Alrighty, now who wants to lick the spoon?" Asked Mom.

"ME!" Yelled Nikki and Jade at the same time. They both looked at each other.

"I said it first!" Yelled Nikki.

"No, I did!" Yelled Jade.

"No, me!"

"No, me!"

"MOMMY!" They both yelled. I rolled my eyes and Mom chuckled.

"How about you *both* lick the spoon." I said, sarcastically.

"Eww! I don't want her germs!" Yelled Nikki.

"Hey! I don't have germs." Said Jade.

"Yeah, you do." Said Nikki.

"Nuh-uh."

"Yuh-huh!"

"Nuh-Uh!"

"Yuh-huh!" Jade picked up some flour and threw it at Nikki.

"Hey!" Yelled Nikki. I laughed and Jade stuck her tongue out at Nikki. Nikki picked up some butter and threw it at me. It landed in my face.

"Nikki!" I said. Nikki laughed.

"What was that for?" I asked her.

"For laughing." Said Nikki. I picked up some sugar and threw it in Nikki's direction, but I missed. It hit mom in the face instead! Mom looked shocked, and so did we.

"Sorry, Mom!" I said. Mom wiped it off of her face, picked up some butter and threw it back at me. Mom, Nikki and I laughed.

"FOOD FIGHT!" Yelled Nikki. The four of us just started throwing ingredients at each other for at least 10 minutes. Soon Dad walked in.

"Hey what's going on—?" Before he could even finish his sentence, someone accidentally threw some flour at him. It landed in his face and hair. He looked shocked and so did we. He wiped some flour out of his face. Jade laughed.

"Daddy looks like a clown!" She yelled. We all laughed. Dad picked up some flour and threw it at mom. Mom looked shocked and threw some back at him. We continued our food fight with Dad.

By the time we were done, there was ingredients all over us and all over the kitchen.

“Alright, now who’s going to help me clean all of this up.” Said Mom. Nikki and I both looked at each other.

“Not it!” We both yelled, putting our fingers on our noses. We both looked at Dad and he put his finger on his nose. Then we looked at Jade.

“Hey! No fair.” Said Jade, crossing her arms. Nikki and I laughed.

“There’s no ‘not it’. All of you are helping me.” Said mom.

“Aww, no fair! Jade started it!” Said Nikki.

“No, you started it!” Said Jade.

“No, you did!”

“No, you did!”

“MOMMY!” They both yelled, again. Mom and I chuckled.

After we were done cleaning the kitchen, the cookies were ready. They tasted good! We got the plate of cookies and turned on a movie and ate them. After the movie was over, we took showers and Jade took a bath so we could get the rest of the food off of us from our little food fight earlier. After I took a shower, I came back to my room and checked my phone again and when I saw my phone, my heart dropped.

I haven’t checked my phone almost at all today, except for when I woke up, and I had even more missed calls and text messages than before! From Jackson, I had 4 missed FaceTime calls, 3 phone calls, 2 voicemails and 10 text messages! The first voicemail said:

“Hey Autumn, it’s Jackson again. I don’t know if you got my first call, but I really need to talk to you about something. Please call me back when you get this message. Bye.”

The second one said:

"Autumn, you haven't answered any of my calls or text messages all day. I really need you to call me! It's important. I'm starting to get worried. If you get this message, please call me!" I started shaking a bit. What was so important that he needed to tell me? I looked at the text messages and this was what they said:

"Autumn, are you getting these?? We need to talk." -12:14pm.

"Autumn"- 12:48pm.

"Srsly we need to talk"-12:49pm.

"Autumn. Are you mad at me??"-1:14pm.

"I need you to talk to me! Please, it's important!"-1:22pm.

"Ok, maybe you're just not near your phone right now. I'll give you some time."-1:31pm.

"Hey, Autumn, it's been almost a whole day and I haven't heard from you, are you ok?"-7:12pm.

"Autumn is everything ok??"-7:15pm.

"Autumn please respond!" -7:19pm.

"Autumn"-7:20pm.

Wow, I don't think I've checked my phone since I woke up! I decided I should send him a text message to let him know I was ok. But I still kind of wasn't in the mood to talk to him about what happened. So, I just sent a single word message.

"Hey." -7:23pm.

While I waited for a response, I checked the other messages. I was even more shocked at the amount of times Serenity tried reaching out to me. From her I had 14 missed FaceTime calls and 12 text messages! I read them.

"AUTUMN ARE YOU UP YET?!"-1:32pm.

"ANSWER THE PHONE"-1:34pm.

"PLEASE" -1:34pm.

"PICK UP ITS IMPORTANT" -1:36pm.

"Why are you ignoring everyone??" -2:11pm.

"PICK UP! ITS ABOUT IVEY" -2:14pm.

"ANSWERRRRRRRRRR"-2:15pm

"AUTUMN"-2:17pm.

"Autumn, it's been all day and nobody's heard from you! We're all rlly worried, especially Jackson."-6:58pm.

"AUTUMN MARIE JOHNSON"-7:03pm.

"Seriously, is everything ok??" -7:10pm.

"Autumn, please pick up! Everyone's worried about you and Jackson thinks you're mad at him."-7:10pm.

"Autummmmmmmnnnnn"-7:12pm.

I was sort of scared, what was so important that they need to talk to me about? I reached out to Serenity too.

"Serenityyyyyyyy"-7:24pm.

I scrolled further and looked at some more messages. From Troy I had 1 missed call and 4 text messages.

"Are you mad at Jackson??" -1:16pm.

"Autumn we need you to respond to someone. Serenity and Jackson need to talk to you about something. Seems important."-1:34pm.

"Autumn you haven't replied to anyone today is everything ok??" -7:15pm.

“Jackson is rlly worried plz call him”-7:17pm.

While I was reading the text messages from Troy, I got another message from Jackson.

“Autumn! Thank God, you’re ok! What happened why haven’t you replied to anyone today? We need to talk about what happened at the dance. Is it ok if I call you?” -7:26pm. I replied this:

“I don’t rlly want to talk about the dance, Jackson. Thanks again for asking me! Other than what happened with Ivey, I ended up having one of the best nights of my life. But I don’t want to talk about how it ended.”-7:26pm. While I waited for another reply, I read what Lauren was trying to say. From her, I had two missed calls and two text messages.

“Autumn, please talk to somebody, Serenity and I need to talk to you about something. It’s about Ivey and it’s kind of urgent. Please call us back!”-2:01pm

“We haven’t heard from you today, are you alright? Please text or call someone back.”-7:12pm.

Suddenly, I got a video call from Serenity and Lauren on a group call. Whatever it is that they want to talk to me about, it must be pretty important by the amount of calls and text messages I got, so I was nervous. I inhaled sharply and exhaled, then hit accept.

“Hey Guys!” I said.

“AUTUMN!” Yelled Serenity.

“We were so worried! Is everything ok?” Asked Lauren. I chuckled.

“Yeah, I’m fine now. I just was doing some stuff with my family and I didn’t really want to talk about the dance or hear anything about Ivey.” I said.

"Well, you're going to wanna hear this!" Said Serenity. I got more nervous.

"What happened?" I asked.

"Do you have social media?" Asked Serenity.

"No, I don't really do social media." I said.

"Hold on a sec, I'm about to send you something." Said Serenity.

What is going on? What does social media have anything to do with the dance? And is it that important? I got a notification from Serenity and it looked like an image. I tapped it and I saw a screenshot of someone's comment section, and these were some really mean people! Here's what some comments said:

"LOLOL SHE LOOK LIKE A CLOWN!"

"It's the hideous dress for me"

"She fell so hard she broke the freaking table?? LOL she really needs to go on a diet!"

"I know her, she's so annoying and kind of deserved it lol"

"Not her trynna steal someone else's bf LOL"

"She's so ugly, why does she think she's better than anyone lol?"

"Stop leaving so many hate comments! I can't like them all ha-ha"

"Sis hair look like it ain't been washed in days"

"She looks like one of those gremlin thingies lolol!"

"AUTUMN!" I heard Serenity yell. I startled for a second. I was so caught up in reading comments, I had almost forgotten that I was on a video call!

"Huh, what?!" I said.

"This is bad! Look what people are saying!" Said Lauren. I was sort of confused, were they talking about me or someone else?

"Wait, who are they talking about?" I asked.

"You Autumn! Ivey recorded you falling into the table and posted it!" Said Serenity. I was shocked! I saw her recording but I didn't think she'd go as low as to POST IT ON THE INTERNET!

"WHAT?!" I yelled.

"It's true! I can send a screenshot of the video on her account." Said Lauren.

My heart sank into my stomach as my phone buzzed again. It was a screenshot from Lauren. I opened it and I saw the screenshot of the video of me at the dance COVERED IN FOOD! And it had 700 views and 500 likes! And the caption said:

"Autumn Johnson. The girl who tried to steal my man. She really thinks she's better than everyone at school and walks around like she owns the place. Now look at her. Nobody tries to tear apart me and my man and get away with it. This is what happens when you mess with me. Now maybe she knows her place lol."

I was in such shock, that I just stared ahead and dropped my phone from out of my hand. After all the stuff that Ivey has put me through since I've been going to school here, now she goes as low as to post an embarrassing video of me at the dance! I don't get it, why does she have to torment me? Why can't she just leave me alone and let me live my life? I wanted to cry. Now people that I don't even know are having fun at my expense and are saying a whole bunch of mean things about me. And not only that, but I have to go back to the torment on Monday when I go back to school.

"Hello, Autumn?" Asked Lauren. I picked up my phone. Serenity and Lauren were still there.

"Autumn, we're so sorry." Said Lauren. I couldn't even bother responding.

"Are you ok?" Asked Serenity. I didn't even want to talk anymore.

"I'll call you guys another time." I said. I quickly hung up before they could say anything else. I through my phone across the room and covered my head with blankets and bawled my eyes out. I heard my phone keep buzzing from across the room, but I didn't get up to see who it was. I just wanted to lay there.

I started to think about everything that had happened to me since we moved states. With Ms. Dobbins and Ivey and her friends, all of the stuff they put me through. Of all of the people in school, why do they feel the need to pick on *me*? What did *I* do? All I did was talk to Jackson and they hated me.

I must not have been keeping track of time, because eventually someone knocked on my door and came in. I didn't bother to look up and see who it was. It was Nikki, based off of the voice.

"Autumn! Mom said do you want the rest of these cookies-" she took a pause.

"Autumn, what's wrong?" She asked. I didn't respond. I didn't really care for cookies at the moment. I heard her exit the room. A couple minutes later I heard someone else come in. It was mom.

"Autumn, what's the matter, sweetie?" She asked. I didn't respond again. She sat down next to me.

"Anything you want to talk to me about?" She asked, again. I decided to just tell my mom what was going on. Maybe she can help me do something about it. I sat up and wiped my eyes a little bit.

"Aw, come here." My mom put her arms around me and gave me a hug. I cried on her shoulder.

"Mom.... remember what happened at the dance yesterday?" I asked, hesitantly.

"Yeah, what about it?" She asked. I paused because I started to cry again.

"It got worse." I said, my voice breaking.

"What do you mean?"

"Ivey posted the video of me falling into the dessert table." My mom stopped hugging me.

"WHAT?!" She yelled.

"The video has 700 views and 500 likes. And the caption on the video and the comments are really mean. Mom, you have no idea of my thoughts and what I should do to her.

"Oh, my gosh Autumn. I want you to always remember and never forget what The Bible says about revenge.

Really, mom?

Well it says, Autumn, Vengeance is Mine. God will take care of it for you.

"But, people I don't even know are making fun of me." I started to get my phone so I could show my mom the screenshots that Serenity and Lauren sent me. My mom took my phone and started reading the caption. Then she scrolled and looked at the screenshot of the comments. Then she turned and looked back at me.

"I just don't get it. What did I ever do to them to make them hate me so much?! I didn't even do anything! All I did was talk to Jackson once and they hated me. Even the teachers hate me!" I said. My mom hugged me again.

"Autumn, you did not have to put up with this abuse on your own. Tomorrow, I'm emailing your principal and I'm going to ask him why he hasn't done anything about this. It's going to be ok." She said.

"It doesn't matter what you do, that video is on the internet! And at least 700 people have seen it already! Now people are really going to bother me in school."

"Autumn, look at me." She said. I looked at her.

"You are an incredibly smart, fun and beautiful little girl. And you are not about to let what Oakley and her friends say about you upset you like this." Said Mom.

"Her name's Ivey not Oakley, mom. And it's not just Ivey and her friends. It feels like.... a lot of people hate me. People laugh at me in class when Ivey insults me. And Ms. Dobbins would act like I'm bothering her when I asked her to move me up again because I couldn't see from where I was sitting. And then the whole class laughed because she was annoyed at me, like they were sharing the same frustration." I explained.

"That doesn't mean that they don't like you, Autumn. As good of a person as you are, I'm sure most of them like you and are just putting on a show for Ivey." Said Mom.

"What do you mean?"

"A lot of kids aren't as strong and independent as you are, they can't handle pressure like you can. So, they do whatever they can to get on the popular kid's good side so they don't end up becoming the target. But you're different, you're not like them. You're not a follower, and that's what they don't like.... You just keep being a leader.... be you!" I smiled.

"Thanks. But I'm still sort of dreading going back to school Monday just for Ivey and the rest of these kids to make me miserable."

"Don't give Ivey that type of power over you. Who is she? She's just a girl you go to school with! Think about it. Where is she going to be after you graduate? Is she even going to matter in 5 years?" I thought for a second. *Is* Ivey going to matter in 5 years?

"Exactly. You're going to get through this eventually. You are an incredible young lady. Remember what we used to say at Church? 'Weeping may endure for a night'...." My mom let me finish.

"'But joy cometh in the morning'." I finished, smiling. My mom patted my back.

"That's my girl. You just keep holding on and being the best you that you can be. Now cheer up, pretty girl." She said. I wiped my tears and took a deep breath.

"Let's go watch another movie. Your dad's putting on a comedy." She said again, laughing. I chuckled and started getting up.

I went downstairs with my family and we watched the movie. The movie *was* funny. After a while, I did my night routine and went to bed. I didn't bother checking my phone. I still really wasn't in the mood.

Chapter 15: Betrayal

Two days later, on Monday, I was really nervous to go back to school. I'm not really worried about Ms. Dobbins that much, but the other kids are probably going to start bothering me because of the video Ivey posted about me.

I walked in and went to my locker. When I opened my locker, another note fell out. I picked it up and unfolded it. Here's what it said:

"I told you to stay away from Jackson. Now maybe I've taught you to stay in a child's place. Love, Ivey. PS, you looked much better with the cake covering your face HAHA"

Suddenly I heard more laughter behind me. I turned around and not only were Ivey and her friends behind me, but so were Tara and a bunch of other kids! Pointing and laughing at me.

"Hey, Autumn! Want some cake?" One of them yelled. Then they all laughed again. I rolled my eyes, crumpled up the note, threw it on the ground and then stormed off. I started heading towards the cafeteria to sit with Serenity and Lauren. After what I'd been through, I definitely needed some hugs and encouragements from them. I sat down at the table.

"Hey girls!" I said. They both stared at me, seemingly with mixed emotions.

"What's wrong?" I asked. They both looked at each other sadly, then back at me. I was confused, and sort of nervous. Why are they being so quiet?

"Is everything ok?" I asked, again. Serenity took a deep breath and exhaled.

"Autumn, we can't be seen together anymore." Said Serenity, bluntly. I was even more confused and shocked. What did she mean we can't be seen together?

"What, why?!" I asked.

"Well.... yesterday, we both talked and we decided that we don't want the same treatments that you're getting from the other kids here." Said Lauren.

"And.... if you end up getting in trouble because of Ivey, we don't want to end up getting in any kind of trouble with the teachers either." Said Serenity. I was in such shock that I couldn't even say anything. These two have been with me since I've been going to school here, and now they're just going to leave while I'm already weak? Is this some sort of joke?!

"We're sorry, Autumn. I hope you understand." Said Lauren.

"No, I don't understand. You two are supposed to be my friends! Friends don't just leave when things get rough!" I said.

"I know, but.... I just wouldn't be able to handle what you're going through. And I don't want Ivey to pick on us too just for being seen with you." Said Lauren. I closed my eyes and took deep breaths, in an attempt to calm down a little bit. When I opened my eyes, Serenity and Lauren were getting up to leave.

"Wow, so you're just going to leave all because you're afraid of what stupid Ivey thinks?!" I demanded.

"We're not scared of Ivey. We just can't be seen with you anymore. You're an outcast." Said Serenity. I looked at them in shock. Are they being serious? After everything they said about how I would always have them no matter how hard middle school can get, they're just going to stop talking to me?

"It was nice knowing you, Autumn." Said Lauren. Then they both left.

I couldn't even process what had just happened. Did my two closest friends from this school just leave me because they were afraid of what Ivey thinks?! Were they even my friends at all?!

I got up and started running. I didn't know where I was going, I just needed to take a walk and comprehend what just happened. As I was running out of the cafeteria, I ran into Jackson and Troy.

"Autumn, there you are—" Troy paused when he saw how upset I looked. They both stared at me.

"What's wrong?" Before I could answer or do anything, Jackson spoke up.

"Uh, Troy.... do you mind giving us a sec?" He asked.

"Yeah, sure." Said Troy, walking away. Jackson gave me a hug, and I started feeling a lot better. Once we were done hugging, we spoke up.

"What happened?" He asked. I was still sort of shocked from what had previously happened, so I didn't bother bringing it up again.

"I'd rather not talk about it. I'm glad you're here!" I said. Jackson paused for a second and looked sort of upset.

"What's wrong?" I asked. Jackson looked at me nervously.

"You're probably going to hate me for saying this but.... we can't talk anymore." He said, nervously. I was shocked. Another friend, LEAVING ME?! What's going on?!

"What?!" I said. I started getting Deja vu from my friendship with Serenity and Lauren coming to an end.

"I'm sorry, Autumn. I tried to tell you over the weekend but.... you didn't answer my calls or texts again."

"So, that's it? You're letting Ivey win?"

“Hey, Jackson! Check this out!” A kid yelled from inside. Jackson started to walk away. I stood there. He stopped and looked back at me. I looked back at him. Then he turned around and headed into the cafeteria. I continued running out of the hallway.

I ended up running outside in the back of the school. I needed to cool off. But I was so angry from what just happened, I kicked the flagpole. It really hurt my foot, but I ignored the pain.

Now, not only is Ivey going to keep making me miserable, but now I don’t even have Serenity, Lauren and Jackson to back me up! Why would they leave me *now*?! Were they really my friends? Because last time I checked, friends are supposed to stay with you when times get rough, not kick you while you’re already down. I guess now I have run this race alone now.

When I heard the bell ring, I straightened myself up and started heading to homeroom.

Once I go to homeroom, I did some studying while I waited for the announcements. A couple minutes later, the announcements came on and everyone stood up for the Pledge of Allegiance. After the Pledge of Allegiance, everyone sat down and some more announcements came on:

“Attention all, we are proud to announce that we will be having our very first school Christmas party on December 18th in the library from 5:00pm-9:00pm. Be sure to wear something that resembles Christmas. Anyone caught wearing anything inappropriate will be removed immediately. Auditions for the Spring musical will be held in the auditorium from Tuesday to Friday. Make sure you sign up on the door of room 103. Will the following students please report to the main office after announcements? Derek Brown, Autumn Johnson. That’s all the announcements for today. Have a great day everyone!”

At first, I was a little confused as to why they were calling me on the announcements again. But then I remembered my mom emailed the principal about Ivey! Oh, boy. I got my stuff up and started to head down to the main office.

Once I got to the principal's office, I knocked on the door.

"Come in!" I heard him say. I opened the door and sat down in the chair in front of his desk.

"Good morning, Autumn." He said.

"Good morning." I said.

"So, over the weekend I received an interesting email from your mom about something that happened at the dance on Friday. Can you tell me what happened?"

"Well.... did anyone tell you that someone fell into the dessert table and it collapsed?"

"Yes. There was a dancing accident I heard."

"No, that was me. And it wasn't an accident. One of the students tripped me and I fell."

"What?!"

"And the person who did it recorded it and put it on their social media. And the video has 700 views and 500 likes."

"Oh, my! I wasn't aware of that. Can you tell me the name of the student?"

I hesitated. If I tell him the name of the student, is he actually going to do something about the problem, or just underplay it and let it happen again? Or is he going to overreact and do something to make Ivey hate me even more?

"Come on, don't be shy. Just tell me." He said. I took a deep breath.

"The two girls recording me were Ivey Sanders and Leah Cartwright. I'm not sure which one of them tripped me, but the video of me is on Ivey's account." I said. He paused for a second.

"Autumn, listen. We have no tolerance for bullying at this school. Next time Ivey and her friends bother you, let me know and we'll all handle it together. Understand?" He said. I nodded my head.

"And let your mom know that this is being taken care of." He said, again.

"Ok!" I said. I was sort of worried about what was going to happen if I told the principal what was going on. Were the other kids going to treat me worse or is this actually going to stop?

"You can head to first period now." He said. I got my belongings and went to first period.

Later that day at lunch, I walked into the cafeteria and I saw Jackson and Troy sitting at Ivey's table! Seriously? After everything we just went through because of her, you're *sitting* with her at lunch? I ignored it and sat down at an empty table.

As I was eating my lunch, I felt something hard hit the back of my head. Then I heard a bunch of kids laughing. I turned around and saw a half-eaten apple laying on the ground. Then I looked up and saw Ivey and her entire table all pointing and laughing at me, except for Jackson and Troy. Those two didn't seem to be paying attention to what happened. I rubbed the back of my head.

"That's what you get for being a snitch!" Yelled Ivey. Then they laughed again. I rolled my eyes and turned back around to finish eating my lunch. I guess this is the new lunch for me, having to sit all by myself and get food thrown at me. Pretty soon, the lunch bell rang and everyone ran to their next period class.

Next period was science. I wasn't really nervous for that class this time because of that talk with Ms. Dobbins that day.

Plus, she hasn't been giving me any real problems since then. Right now, it's Ivey and Zoey that I have to worry about.

As I was walking into the classroom, I felt someone push me into the classroom and I fell.

"MOVE IT, SNITCH! VIP comin' through!" Yelled Ivey, as I felt the push. Then I saw her and Zoey running into the classroom giggling. I scoffed at them, got up and went to my seat.

A couple minutes later, the bell rang for class to start.

"Good afternoon everyone! So, over the weekend I graded your tests from last week, and most of you did a great job! I'm going to give them to you guys so you guys can look over what you did wrong." Said Ms. Dobbins. She started handing out our papers to us.

I was unsure about one question on the back, but I didn't think I did any worse than a 90. When she got to me and handed me my paper, I turned it over and could *not* believe my eyes. I GOT A 45! What did I do wrong?! I looked at my paper and I didn't get any answers wrong on the front, so I looked on the back. I got that one question wrong that I wasn't so sure about, but the directions said that it was only worth 5 points! How did I end up with a 45? I looked back at the front top to make sure it was my paper, and it was. I was confused. Did the 9 just look like a 4 or is that my actual grade?

"Ok, does anyone have any questions before we move on to something else?" Asked Ms. Dobbins. My hand shot up.

"Autumn?" Said Ms. Dobbins. The class turned to look at me.

"I'm confused about my grade. I only got one question wrong and my grade is bad. Is this a mistake?" I said. Ms. Dobbins came over to my desk and looked at my exam.

"Oh, that's not a mistake. You see that star I put up at the top?" She asked.

"Yes?" I said, confused.

"That means that I heard talking on this side of the class. And I don't know if you cheated or not, so I took away 50 points."

"What? But I wasn't cheating!"

"I never said that you were or weren't, but I have to assume that you were if I hear talking on your side of the classroom."

"But I wasn't talking!"

"Autumn, there are other people in this classroom other than you, if you hadn't noticed, we can't just waste this much time because you aren't happy with a grade that *you* got. And if you want to continue this conversation, we can call your mother down here."

Did she seriously just threaten to call my mom because she gave me an F for no reason?! Am I being pranked right now?

"Are we done here?" She asked, again. I stared at her for couple seconds trying to process what just happened. Finally, I spoke up.

"Ok...." But I wasn't happy about it. She nodded and walked away. I looked forward and saw Ivey and Zoey, who were sitting in front of me, turned around snickering at me, as if to tease me. I rolled my eyes and they both turned around.

"Alright class, so today we're just going to be watching a sci-fi. And pay close attention, because some of the points in this film are going to be on your next quiz." Said Ms. Dobbins to the class. I got out my notebook so I could copy some stuff down. Then she turned the movie on.

In the film, the doctors were trying to figure out a patient's blood type. And the doctors made a mistake in judgement and based off of how I was looking at it, the patient's blood type was AB+, but the doctors concluded AB-.

"Wait, if the blood tested positive for the RH balance, then that would make his blood type AB positive, not negative." I commented aloud. Zoey turned around.

"No dip, Sherlock." She snorted. The class laughed at her comment. I don't really know why, but it really irritated me when she said that. I was already having kind of a bad day, and now she's being sarcastic with me? All because I knew an answer.

"Why don't you just leave me alone? Just because you didn't think of it sooner doesn't mean you get to say whatever you want." I yelled at her.

"Autumn, step outside." Said Ms. Dobbins. I was confused. Why is she singling me out again? Zoey said something to me first!

"Why?" I asked.

"Don't ask me 'why', just step outside." Said Ms. Dobbins. I stood up, walked outside the classroom, shut the door and waited. A couple seconds later, Ms. Dobbins came outside and shut the door.

"Do you mind telling me what just happened?" Asked Ms. Dobbins.

"All I was saying that the doctors in the film made a mistake and Zoey said, 'no dip, Sherlock'." I said.

"Well, why were you talking in class?"

"I wasn't really 'talking', it was more like thinking aloud." Suddenly, the principal started walking down the hallway.

"It doesn't matter. I just wish you would be quiet in my class! I'm so sick and tired of you being a nuisance and always causing trouble. You continue to disrupt my classroom and then get upset when someone calls you out on it. That's not how life works. In the real world, Autumn, people take responsibility for their actions." Said Ms. Dobbins.

Where the heck did that come from? This started off as basically a normal conversation, and now all of a sudden since the principal is walking this way, she wants to make this big scene like I'm the problem kid?

"I *do* take responsibility for my actions!" I said.

"Do you really?" Said Ms. Dobbins. I raised one eyebrow in confusion.

The principal walked toward us.

"Woah, what's going on here?" He asked.

"Just typical Autumn, starting more trouble in my class again." Said Ms. Dobbins.

Typical?! What does she mean typical? I don't always start trouble in her class! Is she *trying* to get me in trouble with the principal?

"Autumn, why don't you step inside my office?" Said the principal. Are you freaking kidding me?! Now I'm being sent to the office just because Ms. Dobbins overreacted!

"But I-" Ms. Dobbins interrupted me again.

"No buts, just go to the office!" Said Ms. Dobbins. I was in such shock I didn't even really know what to do! Is this actually happening? I feel like I'm in a twilight zone. I eventually decided to just go to the office with the principal.

"Oh, and by the way you're getting written up and I might just be calling your mother!" Yelled Ms. Dobbins, as I walked away. I rolled my eyes and continued walking. Once we got there, I sat down in the seat in front of his desk. He sat down in his chair.

"So, explain to me what happened back there." He said.

"All I said was that the characters in the movie we were watching made a mistake and someone got sarcastic with me because I knew the answer. And, I'm already having a bad day, so I'm already irritated-" He interrupted me.

"Wait, Wait. Who were you talking to when you said that?"

"No one, really. I was just thinking aloud."

"Ok. And then what happened?"

"So, then I told the student to leave me alone and that just because she didn't think of the answer sooner didn't mean she could insult me. And then Ms. Dobbins asked me to step outside."

"Ok, Autumn. Let me just tell you this. You know you're not supposed to be talking in class."

"Yes."

"So, when you started talking during the movie, maybe it was distracting to the student and maybe that's why she reacted the way she did. And maybe Ms. Dobbins asked you to step outside so that you wouldn't be a distraction to other students."

I thought for a second. It made sense when he said it, but that's not why Zoey said that to me. She only said it because she wanted to have something negative to say to me. And Ms. Dobbins asking me to step out instead of both of us is her singling me out again! And she didn't end up getting that mad until the principal came.

"I guess that makes sense.... But before you started walking down the hallway towards us, our conversation started off like an ordinary conversation. Then when she saw you, she completely flipped out on me." I said.

"Why do you think she did that?" He asked.

"Because she hates me."

"And you think that because?"

"I don't know why, but Ms. Dobbins singles me out a lot in class. Even if I'm not the one starting the argument, she'll still find *some* reason, even if it doesn't make any sense."

"Well, I'm sure she doesn't 'hate' you, Autumn. But I definitely will check up with her on what you just said. But in the meantime, no more talking in class when the teacher says not to. Ok?"

"I see what you mean. I'll try to be quieter." Just then, the bell rang for next period.

"Ok, you can go ahead to next period." Said the principal.

"Thanks!" I said, getting my book bag. I walked out of his office and headed to my next period.

Chapter 16: Not My Fault

I rode the bus home alone today since Lauren doesn't want to sit by me anymore in public. What a day! When I got home, I threw my book bag on the couch and plopped down. My mom came in the living room.

"Hey, Autumn! How was school?" She asked.

"Horrible." I said. She sat down next to me and gave me a hug.

"It's ok, sweetie." She said, rubbing my back. I started tearing up again.

"Do you want to talk about it?" She asked. I really needed someone to vent to, so I started telling her about my day.

"Well, for starters.... when I first walked in there was a note in my locker from Ivey saying that she told me to stay away from Jackson and maybe now I know to stay in a child's place and that.... I looked better with the cake in my face.... and then I heard people laughing behind me asking me did I want any cake, to mock the fact that I fell into a dessert table. Then, Serenity, Lauren and Jackson all told me that they can't be seen with me anymore in public...." I paused for a second.

"Isn't Jackson the one you went to the dance with?"

"Yes.... and he's embarrassed to be seen with me now because of Ivey. And Serenity and Lauren said they don't want other kids to bother them for being seen with me. But it's cool though.

"Well, if they're too embarrassed to be seen with you now, then they weren't your friends from the beginning."

"You'll make new friends! It just takes time." I took a pause. I guess if they won't have my back at my lowest, then they didn't deserve me at my best.

"Did anything else happen today?" Asked Mom.

"Oh, yeah. That was just the start of my day! So, then in homeroom I got called down to the principal's office and the principal was telling me that he didn't know I was the one who broke the dessert table and that they have a zero tolerance for bullying and he would take care of this. So, I guess he must've said something to Ivey because then at lunch, someone threw a half-eaten apple at my head and then Ivey called me a snitch and everyone at her table started laughing except Jackson and his friend Troy, who coincidentally are now sitting with Ivey and her friends. And then, just before science class, Ivey and her friend pushed me into the classroom and yelled at me to move saying she was VIP, and then-" my mom stopped me.

"Hold up, hold up. Did you just say someone pushed?!" She demanded.

"Yeah! And then she called herself VIP."

"Wait, what is VIP? Is that some sort of bit you guys do in science class?" I rolled my eyes.

"No, she was just being sarcastic."

"And you let her push you?" I raised up an eyebrow at her. What did she mean "let her", I didn't even see her coming!

"I *didn't* 'let her' push me, I didn't see her until she walked by."

"I mean you didn't push her back or at least tell anybody?"

"Not yet, and what's the point? Just for them to find some lame excuse to blame me. And if I push her back, then *I'll* get in trouble."

"Don't worry about getting in trouble. If you do, let me handle that. But you *never* let someone put their hands on you and get away with it. Understand?" I nodded.

"And I'll be talking to the principal about that, too. Anything else happen today?"

"After that, I received my science test back and Ms. Dobbins took away 50 points from my test because she heard talking on my side of the classroom and then when I told her I wasn't talking she threatened to call you if I kept going with it."

"She gave you a failing grade over something you didn't do?!"

"Yes, but that's not all! Then, when we were watching a movie today, one of the doctors in the movie made a mistake and when I said it aloud someone got all sarcastic and said, 'no dip, Sherlock'. And then when I said something back to her, Ms. Dobbins told me to go step outside. So when I was telling her what happened and that I wasn't talking to her, I was thinking aloud, the principal started walking our way and then Ms. Dobbins completely overreacted and started going on and on about how much she wishes I would just be quiet in her class and stop being a nuisance and in the real world people take responsibility for their actions-"

"Wait, hold on! Did she call the principal down there or something?" I started getting annoyed at how many times she interrupted me, but I answered her questions anyway, because she's my mom.

"I don't know! Maybe he was just walking through checking on people. But then when Ms. Dobbins saw him, her mood completely changed! It's almost like she *wanted* me to get in trouble!"

"Why would she want you to get in trouble?"

"Ms. Dobbins is my science teacher that I was telling you about! The one who makes that class really hard for me."

"Ok, keep going."

"So, the principal took me to his office and was telling me that I wasn't supposed to be talking in class and all. So, I told him about Ms. Dobbins and how she hates me and it seems like she singles me out, so he said he would talk to her. And that's pretty much it." My mom thought for a second.

"Ok, tonight I'm emailing your principal and Ms. Dobbins and I'm getting to the bottom of this." She said.

"But what if Ms. Dobbins starts treating me worse because you told on her?" I asked.

"You shouldn't be worried about that! She's a teacher. If she does start treating you worse, let me handle it. It's going to be okay...." Said Mom. Boy, I really hope she's right. I feel like I'm slowly going crazy with everything happening.

"I sure hope so." I said. My mom gave me another hug.

A couple minutes later, Nikki and Jade came home, so we went into the kitchen to get an after-school snack. After we were done, we started working on our homework. I had a worksheet for Algebra, a passage to read and some questions to answer for American History. I decided to do Algebra first, since it was less work than American History. After I was done Algebra, I moved onto American History. When I was about halfway done, my mom called me into the living room.

"Autumn, come here for a couple minutes." She said. I got up and went in the living room to my mom.

"Yes?" I asked.

"So, I was emailing your principal again about what was going on, and he told me that what you're going through isn't anything personal against you." I was confused. What did she mean it isn't personal?

"What do you mean?" I asked.

"So, he's telling me that right now, that mean teacher of yours is going through a lot in her own life. So, maybe when she sees how happy you look it upsets her."

I raised up an eyebrow. I mean, don't get me wrong, it's a shame that Ms. Dobbins is going through a rough time, but she should at least be professional enough to put her emotions aside when it comes to students. And what does her personal life have to do with me at all? It's not *my* fault.

"Of course, I'm not excusing her behavior towards you, but could you try being a little bit more understanding? Maybe it's not intentional, maybe it's just subconscious. And maybe, what you're going through with Ivey and those other girls is the same situation. They could be going through something in their personal lives and could be subconsciously taking it out on you." Said Mom.

"But why me specifically? There are other kids besides me in school. It's a shame that something might be going on in their lives, but why do they have to take it out on *me* of all people?" I asked.

"Well, maybe they're jealous of you. You're a smart girl, you're pretty, kind, and fun. And you have good friends and a stable family, and you live in a good environment. Not a lot of kids get that, you know." Said mom.

"Had! I HAD good friends."

"Autumn, you're missing the point. I'm not saying that what they're doing to you is ok or that they have a right to act this way. But you could also try having compassion on them. It may not be intentional. Maybe they just see you and the wonderful life that *you* have, and it makes them wonder 'what's so great about her?'"

"Is that why people say that I think I'm better than everyone?"

"Maybe that's why!" I thought for a second. Maybe Mom's right. Maybe what some people are going through in their own lives is affecting how they act in school. But it's not my fault! I'm not the reason for what they're going through at home. Why do they feel the need to break me down? Is it because it makes them feel better? Can they not just express their anger on their own?

"Anyway, the principal says he's going to talk to Ms. Dobbins about what happened and he's going to talk to Ivey and some other kids about someone pushing you. Ok?" Said mom.

"Ok." I said.

"Now, go ahead and finish your homework." Said mom. I went back in the kitchen to finish my homework. I hope the principal doesn't do something *too* outrageous tomorrow. It was me telling on Ivey that made her madder to begin with. Oh well, I guess I'll just have to wait till tomorrow to find out.

Chapter 17: Torment

The next day, in homeroom, the morning announcements came on and everyone stood up for the Pledge of Allegiance. After the Pledge of Allegiance, some announcements came on.

"Attention all, we are proud to announce that we will be having our very first school Christmas party on December 18! Be sure to wear something that resembles Christmas. Anyone caught wearing anything inappropriate be removed immediately. Auditions for the Spring musical will be held in the auditorium from Tuesday to Friday. Make sure you sign up on the door of room 103. Will the following students please report to the main office after announcements? Autumn Johnson, Ivey Sanders, Zoey McCarthy, Eric Gimble, Serenity Michaels, Kaylee Wilson, Jacob Anderson. That's all the announcements for today. Have a great day everyone!"

Uh oh! This must be about Ivey pushing me. My heart dropped. And I think the other kids he called, including Serenity and Zoey, are just kids in the class that might've seen what happened. I just hope the principal doesn't make a big fuss out of it and make them hate me even more.

I got up and started heading to the main office. When I got there, I went into the principal's office. Only one person was there already besides me, so we waited a couple minutes. Once everyone was there, the principal closed the door.

"Alright, let's get to the bottom of this. I'm hearing that there's been numerous incidents of bullying going on with certain kids. And if you've been going to this school for a while, you'll know that we have a zero tolerance for bullying. But now I'm hearing of a physical interaction between two kids. Now, Autumn. I'm going to ask you this. What physical interactions have been made with you and Ivey on Monday?" He said.

I did a face palm. Why would he ask me something like that in front of Ivey and Zoey? Now that Ivey and Zoey know that I told on them, they're going to treat me worse. Nice job, principal.

Everyone turned to look at me, so I hesitated. But then, I just decided to speak up.

"Well, first off.... at lunch, I felt a half-eaten apple hit the back of my head.... And when I looked.... Ivey and most of her table were laughing and pointing in my direction." I explained. The principal nodded.

"Anything else?" He asked. I hesitated, again.

"Go ahead, don't be shy." He said. I took a pause, and then continued.

"And then.... on the way into science class.... I felt someone push me into the classroom.... and Ivey yelled at me to move because 'VIP' was coming through.... and she called me a snitch too...." I said, hesitantly. The principal nodded.

"Is that all?" He asked. I thought for a second.

"Well, I think that's all the *physical* interactions between us since the night at the dance." I said. The principal looked over at Ivey.

"Ivey, did you or anyone at your table throw something at Autumn yesterday?" He asked.

"No." Said Ivey. I almost fell out of my seat! She's seriously going to stand there and LIE right to everyone's faces?! I KNOW someone threw an apple at me!

"Did you or Zoey tell Autumn that you were 'VIP' or call her a 'snitch'?" He asked. Ivey started tearing up.

"No...." She said, starting to cry. Seriously? Now, she's shedding crocodile tears! Where were those tears at when she was tormenting me since the day I arrived here?

"And did you or Zoey put your hands on Autumn at all yesterday?" He asked her.

"No, I would never do that!" She said, crying even more. Oh.... my.... gosh. Is this actually happening?! I really hope that the principal isn't buying any of this! She's obviously crying to get out of a punishment, or to get sympathy! The principal looked at Zoey.

"What about you, Zoey? Did you see anything?" He asked. Of course, Zoey isn't going to say anything! She's friends with the girl! Why even bother asking?

"No." She said. I knew it! The principal looked at Serenity.

"How about you, Serenity?" He asked. Serenity hesitated. Oh, no. Don't tell me she's about to lie for Ivey, too. She already stopped being friends with me for her....

"Go ahead, you can tell me." He said. Serenity paused.

"Well, I thought I heard someone saying 'VIP comin' through', but I don't think I saw anything else." She answered. Well, that's sort of a relief. At least the principal knows I'm not crazy!

"Oh?" Commented the principal.

"Yeah, but there were actually multiple times when Ivey did something to Autumn. Once, she threw a paper ball at the back of Autumn's head in science class. So, I asked why they don't just leave her alone, and they told me to mind my own business. And another time, where she poured a smoothie down her shirt." Explained Serenity. Thank you! At least Serenity knows the truth when it comes to the principal. But how is she and Lauren going to act when it comes to the other kids? Ivey stepped forward.

"None of that is true! Both of those stories are lies!" She yelled, crying. Zoey pulled her arm back in an attempt to restrict her. The principal ignored her and looked at another kid.

“Ok, Eric. How about you? Did you see anything?” He asked.

“No.” He answered. Stupid Eric. The principal looked at another student

“What about you, Kaylee?” He asked.

“No.” She answered. Forget you, Kaylee. The principal looked at the last student.

“Jacob, what about you?” He asked.

“No.” He answered. Whatever, Jacob. The bell rang for everyone to go to first period.

“Thank you everyone, you guys can go ahead to first period now.” Said the principal. Everyone ran out of the principal’s office.

“Wait, Autumn!” He yelled out. I stopped and turned back around.

“I’d just like to let you know that I talked to Ms. Dobbins about that failing grade and she said she’s going to let you retake it next week. And I will be emailing your mom tonight about that and about what’s going on with you and Ivey. Ok?” He said.

“Ok!” I said.

“You can go ahead to class now.” He said. I walked out of his office and closed the door.

When I walked out of the main office, Ivey and all of her friends were standing in the hallway across from the office, giving me the death stare. I ignored them and walked off. When I continued walking, more people throughout the hallway were also stopping to stare at me. I was confused. How many people did she tell already? I started walking quicker and went into the classroom for first period.

Later that day, 4th period was Study Hall. I walked into the classroom and there were a lot of new people that I didn't really remember being in this class with me. And some of those people were Ivey, Leah, Zoey and Sandra! What's going on? Why are there so many people in here? When the bell rang, everyone ran to a seat.

"Ok, class. I know it may look different in here today. But that's because today we're having a combined class while Mr. Brown is out sick." Announced Mr. Lee. Oh, no! That means I have to put up with Ivey and her friends along with Tara for a whole class period?! With no backup?! What am I going to do? I can't handle all five of them on my own!

"Anyway, class will operate just like any class. Work on something from another class. And if you want to, you can talk to people around you, just as long as it doesn't get too noisy in here. Ok, get started!" He said, again.

I don't want to have to put up with them for a whole class period! But then again, I won't have to worry about them if I'm not listening to them! I quickly yanked out my headphones from my book bag and put them on and started listening to music as I did my work.

After about 10 minutes of me doing classwork, I looked up and saw Ivey and Leah standing in front of my desk annoyed. It looked like they were saying something, but I couldn't hear them because my music was kind of loud. I took off my headphones.

"Can I help you?" I asked, annoyed.

"Do you mind not singing? You're hurting my ear drums!" Said Ivey. Singing? I wasn't singing. Wait, was I?

"What are you talking about?" I asked.

"You're singing along to your music. And it's distracting, so knock it off!" Yelled Leah. I was so into my classwork that I didn't even realize I was singing along! Whoops!

"Oh, my bad! I'll be quieter." I said. They both flipped their hair and walked away. I put my headphones back on and started working on my classwork.

About ten more minutes passed when I looked up and saw Ivey and Leah standing in front of my desk *again* with the same expression on their face as last time. I figured I must've been subconsciously singing along to my music again not paying attention. I took off my headphones.

"Yes?" I asked.

"You're still singing! Shut up!" Yelled Ivey.

"My bad!" I said, again. They both walked away again.

I decided this time to not put my headphones in again in case I started singing along again. And plus, Ivey and her friends seemed too preoccupied with whatever they're doing to bother me. So, seems like I'm in the clear. I just decided to work on my classwork.

After about five minutes, I heard Ivey and her friends singing along to a song. I figured if *they* were singing along to a song, it'd be fine if I listened to *my* music. And maybe it wouldn't really matter if I started singing along. I put my headphones back in and started working on some more classwork.

About 10 minutes later, someone yanked off my headphones and I heard Ivey yelling at me. I looked over at her and she and Leah were standing on the side of me annoyed by something. What could they *possibly* want this time?!

"What was that?" I asked.

"I said will you *please* stop it with the music?! Not only are you singing along again, but this time I can hear it blasting through your headphones! It's annoying!" Yelled Ivey. Weren't they just flat out singing a song? And as noisy as it is in here, how come they're more distracted by me? Just leave me alone.

"Seriously? There's all of this noise in here and you're worried about me?" I asked.

"Yes! We don't like you!" Said Leah. I raised up an eyebrow at her. I already know she doesn't like me; she doesn't have to specify it.

"Well, weren't *you* guys just full on singing?" I asked.

"At least we *can* sing. Unlike you, who sounds like a dying cat!" Yelled Ivey. The people on our section of the classroom started laughing.

"I know, right! I'm surprised my ears aren't bleeding." Commented Tara. I rolled my eyes. I may not be the *best* singer, but I don't sound like a dying cat! And who asked Tara to jump in the conversation?

"Nobody asked you, Tara." I said.

"Oh, shut up. You pathetic piece of trash." Said Tara. The people on our side of the class started oohing at that comment.

"Is that really your only comeback?" I asked.

"Well, maybe *you're* a comeback!" Said Sandra. Uh, what now? Was that meant to be an insult. I chuckled at her and the rest of the class got quiet.

"Please just let *us* do the trash talking." Tara mumbled to Sandra. At this point, nearly the entire class was listening!

"Maybe if you guys didn't worry so much about flirting with boys and bringing down other people, you guys could focus more on making sure you make sense when you talk." I said.

"And maybe if you would just stop walking around like you're better than everyone, which you're not, then you would actually have some friends." Said Ivey. The class started saying "ooh" again at her comment. Is she serious?! How dare she bring up the fact that my friends don't wanna be seen with me anymore!

"Yeah. And you have the nerve to think you're somebody, puh-lease! You're nothing more than an annoying spoiled rat." Said Leah. Everyone started laughing with her.

"Seriously? I'm a spoiled brat now?" I asked.

"I said 'spoiled RAT' not 'spoiled brat'. Go get your ears cleaned out." Said Leah. Everyone laughed again. At that point, I had just decided to ignore them. They obviously just wanted a reaction out of me, and they're not even worthy of getting one. I just put my hoodie up and continued my classwork.

"Yeah, that's right, freak! Go ahead and do your schoolwork like a good girl. Said Tara. The class laughed again.

"I still don't see why she wants to go to school here! Nobody wants her here and literally everyone hates her! I'm so sick her. Just go back to Phoenix and bug the people there." Said Ivey. I rolled my eyes, took a deep breath and continued my classwork. Ivey fanned in front of her face with her hand.

"Oh, my gosh! Was that your breath? Haven't you ever heard of toothpaste?" She asked. The class laughed even harder. I started getting mad, but I continued working on my assignment anyway. I don't even really feel like arguing with them. I am trying really hard not to respond to these idiots.

“Look, now she’s run out of things to say and she’s just going to sit there with her hideous outfit and not say anything.” Said Leah.

“Maybe instead of walking around with your nose in the air, you should be worried about your hair. It looks like it hasn’t been washed for weeks!” Said Tara. The class laughed.

“Tara! Don’t tell her that. She’ll just run to the principal and say ‘mehhh everyone’s bullying me mehhhh’!” Said Ivey, mocking me. Everyone laughed again. Did she seriously just bring up the fact that I told the principal about how she’s treating me?! I almost jumped up out of my seat and told her off. But I decided to just try to tune her out.

“And look, she’s still not saying anything! She’s just sitting there looking bloated!” Said Leah. Everyone laughed again.

“Like, seriously! How did she break an *entire* table with just one fall! Try laying off the carbs, sweetheart.” Said Tara. Everyone laughed again.

“Yeah! Go lose some weight, fatty!” Said Sandra. She bumped Ivey.

“That was good, right?” She asked.

“I guess for *you*.” She said, back.

“And don’t even get me started on her art! I mean it’s good.... for a kindergartener.” Said Tara. Everyone laughed again.

Seriously?! Now they’re coming at my art?! I remember some time earlier in the month, she was the one who told me I was such a good artist! How stupid was I to trust her with what I said about Ivey? I started getting tired of sitting back taking the hits like a coward! I looked up at them and wanted to say something, but I couldn’t put what I wanted to say in real words. Tara looked at me.

"What are you looking at, lardo?" She said to me. Then everyone laughed even harder. I rolled my eyes and continued working on my classwork.

"Exactly, that's what I thought! Go lose some weight and then we'll talk." She said, again. Everyone started saying "ooh" at her again. Is she challenging me or something? Who does she think she is?

"Maybe someone should throw another cake in her face so we don't have to keep looking at.... that." Ivey said, motioning to my face. Everyone laughed even harder. I rolled my eyes again.

"And look at her, she's *still* sitting there. You know what-!" Leah got interrupted by someone yelling something across the room. I couldn't really understand what they said, but everyone started dying of laughter. I looked up and it was Zoey screaming at me from across the room! Great, now all 5 of them are ganging up on me! Why won't they just let me be?!

"What?" I asked her.

"I said just get out of here! Nobody likes you!" She yelled, again. Why is she screaming something like that from across the room?

"Like seriously! She's still sitting here like we want her here!" Said Leah. Suddenly, I lost it and jumped up out of my seat. I couldn't stand sitting there in silence and letting them say whatever they want about me.

"WHY DONT YOU GUYS JUST LEAVE ME ALONE AND LET ME DO MY WORK?! I'm so sick and tired of you guys saying and doing whatever you want to me!" I yelled.

"THEN LEAVE IF YOU DONT LIKE IT!" They all yelled.

"Nobody wants you here. Not even the teachers want you here! You're just wasting space for kids who are actually worthy of going to school here! You'll never be anything but a dumb, fat, ugly, annoying little girl and yet you still continue to walk around the school thinking you're better than everyone. JUST GET OUT!" Yelled Zoey.

"I DO NOT walk around like that. Plus, I shouldn't have to leave, this is my school just as much as it is yours. And just because you guys can't stand the fact that someone is *friends* with someone Ivey likes-!" Zoey interrupted me.

"Oh, my gosh! HE DOESNT EVEN LIKE YOU! How clear does he have to make that?" She yelled.

"There she goes again, thinking she's wanted here!" Said Tara.

"And we would still be a couple if you didn't get in the way! But NOOOO, you just *had* to have someone love you so much that you would get in the way of such a beautiful relationship!" Said Ivey. Is she being serious? She and I both know her and Jackson were never a couple. "Oh my goodness, this girl is delirious." I said.

"Ivey, why don't you stop lying? We both know good and well you guys were never a couple. You can't just like something and call it yours when it isn't!" I said.

"OK, YOU KNOW WHAT-?!" Yelled Ivey, starting to get closer to me. Leah grabbed her arm.

"Don't, it's not worth it." She said.

"BUT SHE'S SO ANNOYING-!" Leah interrupted Ivey.

"It's ok, I know." She said, hugging her. I don't really know why but seeing someone get *that* angry just by my presence was really annoying and embarrassing. Mr. Lee walked over to us. Geez, took him long enough!

"Girls, I don't know what *this* is about, but you guys can discuss whatever this is outside of class! Because right now there are other kids here that are trying to focus on getting things done." He said.

"Well, tell Autumn to leave us alone! She started it!" Said Ivey.

"Are you for real? I didn't start this! I was just trying to do my work and you two started bugging me about my music!" I said.

"Ok, once again. I don't know, nor do I care what's going on here, but please quiet down so other people can concentrate on their work." He said. Then he walked away to start calming down the other kids.

"This has got to be a joke." I said, doing a face palm.

"You know what-" Zoey was interrupted by the bell ringing. Everyone started getting up to leave.

"Finally, now we can get away from her!" Said Tara. They got up and left. I stayed. I didn't even feel like getting up to leave after what just happened.

I put my head down on the desk. I'm so tired of being treated the way I do. All because Ivey can't stand the fact that I talked to a boy she liked! I don't get it, why don't they just leave me alone and let me go to school in peace? I'm here for the same reason *they're* here; to get my education! Why do they feel the need to make school so hard for me? I just want to enjoy middle school like everybody else!

Suddenly, I felt someone touch my shoulder. I figured maybe it was Mr. Lee about to tell me to go to my next class. But I looked up and it was Troy! I don't think I even realized he was in the class the whole time! He gave me a hug.

"Thanks." I said.

"No problem. And don't listen to them. They don't know what they're talking about. We do want you here." He said.

"They *were* right about one thing. No one likes me." I said, starting to cry again.

"That's not true. Remember, Jackson even said himself that he wasn't dating Ivey and that he likes you."

"Well, it sure doesn't seem like it now. He doesn't even want to be seen with me anymore. No one does."

"Well, I don't know what his problem is all of a sudden. But I do know he really likes you."

"But what about Serenity and Lauren?"

"Forget them, too." He said. I chuckled.

"That's the smile I was looking for." He said. I smiled, again. Mr. Lee started walking towards us.

"Ok guys wrap it up. This is my lunch break." He said. Then he walked away. Troy and I started getting our stuff together so we could leave.

"I have Spanish right now, so I'm going the other way. But I just wanted you to know that I wouldn't just not talk to you without an explanation. And if you ever need to talk or vent to someone, just give me a call." Said Troy. I smiled at him.

"Thanks, Troy." I said.

"Anytime." He said. Then he walked out the door and went down the hall. Well, I guess at least *one* person doesn't hate me. I'm really not alone. I picked up my book bag and went to my next period class.

Chapter 18: Payback

At lunch today I was sitting alone, again. I got my lunch at the register and sat down at an empty table and started eating. I peered over at Ivey's table and I didn't see Jackson or Troy! Then I looked around the cafeteria, and I didn't see them anywhere. Where were they? I looked back over at Ivey's table and then Zoey looked at me. I quickly looked away so she wouldn't stop to say anything to me.

"What are you looking at?" She shouted. Everyone at her table laughed. Oh, great. Here we go again.

"Oh, my gosh! She's so annoying, earlier she kept on singing with her music and I was like 'please! My ears'!" Said Ivey, loudly. Everyone at her table laughed again. I turned around and put my hoodie up again.

"Ugh, I feel like hitting her sometimes." I mumbled.

I looked behind me and saw Tara walking past my table, on her way from the lunch line. Uh oh, did she hear me?

"I still don't see why she doesn't just transfer; nobody here likes her." Said Ivey. I don't know what it was, but something about that comment just ticked me off even more. I stood up and started walking to her table.

"Why are you guys so focused on me? I shouldn't have to transfer! I'm here for the same reason *you're* here!" I said. Actually you make me feel like a celebrity because you speak about me all the time.

"Don't come into our personal space! We don't know where you've been!" Said Zoey. Then everyone at the table laughed again.

"You guys really need to grow up, we are in middle school?!" I said.

"We don't like you! Seriously, how many times are we going to have to say that to her?" Said Leah.

"Funny how *all* of you don't like me because of one person. And the reason *she* doesn't like me is because she's mad that I talked to Jackson." I said.

"WOAH, HOLD ON!" They all started saying.

"We don't like you because you *think* Jackson likes you! We were perfectly happy in our relationship before you came along." Said Ivey.

"What relationship? Jackson said you guys weren't even really dating!" I said.

"OK! Just go back to your own table! No one wants you over here! You're always starting trouble! Just leave us alone." Said Zoey. I glared at her for a second, then walked back to my table. As I walked away, I heard someone mumble something and everyone laughed. I ignored them and walked back to my table to finish my lunch.

Soon, the bell rang and everyone ran to their next period class.

Later that day, last period, was science class. Great! Now after the horrific day I've already had, I get to top it all off with some more torment from Ms. Dobbins! Once everyone got to class, the bell rang and everyone went to a seat.

"Ok, class. So, I have an announcement to make. We will be having a project that is due a week after you guys return from Christmas break. But don't worry, you guys won't have to work on it during break. We're just getting started earlier because there's a lot to cover. It will be based off of the movie that we watched yesterday." Said Ms. Dobbins. Oh, no! The movie! I didn't even get to finish it yesterday because of that charade with Zoey and Ms. Dobbins.

"Now, here are the rubrics, score sheets and instructions on what to do for your project. But if you have any questions, feel free to ask." She said, again. Ms. Dobbins started going around handing out sheets to people. I raised my hand. Once she got to my desk, she looked at me.

"Yes, Autumn? You have a question?" She asked.

"Well, it's just that I wasn't here to see the rest of the movie. So, is there a way I could watch it online or at my own house?" I asked her.

"Well, most of the project is based off of the types of blood work tests the doctors run, which you saw already before you left. But if you need help with anything, you can always ask a friend." She said.

"What if she doesn't have any friends?" Yelled out Ivey. Everyone's started laughing again. Right when she said that I felt like going off. How many times is she going to bother me in *one day*?!

"No one was talking to you, Ivey." I said.

"Ivey, Autumn. Enough of this. We have a really tight schedule today, and I'm not about to waste it listening to you two bickering like you're 5 years old." Said Ms. Dobbins. Well, at least *this* time she said something to both of us, and not just me.

"Yeah, we should-" I assumed Ivey was about to say something insulting again, so I interrupted her before she did.

"Oh, shut up Ivey." I said. Everyone started saying "ooh" at me as Ivey turned around to look at me.

"I was about to say that we should not be arguing over something so frivolous." She said to me. I must say, I was shocked to hear something that intelligent coming from someone as small-minded as Ivey.

"Oh, my bad. I didn't know." I said. She flipped her hair and turned back around. Ms. Dobbins came and stood in front of my desk.

"And don't go running to the principal and to your mom saying that everyone's bullying you when everyone knows that you're the one who starts everything." She said. Excuse me?! I don't start *everything*! I admit, I was in the wrong here, but at least I'm mature enough to admit that, unlike Ivey. She was probably just mad that my mom emailed the principal about everything she's been putting me through.

Ms. Dobbins walked away and went back to the front of the class.

"Ok, class. Go ahead and get started on your research. Feel free to talk to people around you, but just keep the volume to a minimum." She said. Then she sat down in her seat. I got started on answering the questions first for my project.

Eventually, I got to this question that said, "How did the doctors find out that the RH balance was incorrect?" I didn't even see that part of the movie because I left right after I pointed out that they messed up. I decided to just skip over it at that point and get back to it later. But then, I realized every question after it had something to do with the part of the movie I didn't watch! I raised my hand. Ms. Dobbins came to me.

"Yes, Autumn?" She asked.

"So, like I was saying earlier, I didn't see the rest of the movie and the questions are based off of the part I didn't see. Is there a way I could watch online or something?" I asked.

"Well the movie isn't online, so I guess you can just think of the questions in terms of science. How would you predict it?" Said Ms. Dobbins.

I looked at my paper again and was confused. When you're handling blood work, whether or not the RH balance was positive or negative, it wouldn't affect the patient. It only affects the patient depending on the blood type, unless it's AB, so either way you wouldn't really know. So how would they discover something like that unless they tested again?

"So, did they run another test or something in the movie because-" Ms. Dobbins interrupted me.

"Wait, slow down, Autumn. You're obviously very confused because the questions you're asking don't even make sense." She said. "Of course, I'm confused! I didn't see the movie." I said.

"Ok, calm down Autumn. What exactly is it that you're confused on?" "Umm.... everything?!" The class laughed at my comment.

"It's really not that hard to understand, Autumn. See if the doctors were working with the blood work and they concluded AB negative, but the real answer is AB positive, how do you think they found out?" She asked, sort of frustrated. I thought for a second.

"I guess the only way they *could've* found out is by running another test." I said. "Now, explain your answer."

"Well, if they would've still given the patient AB positive blood and he's AB negative, it wouldn't make a difference, and that's what I'm confused about."

"Great, then you're on the right track. Now pipe down so other people can concentrate." She said, walking away. I rolled my eyes at her as she walked away.

The next question was "what did they discover about the doctors at the end of the film." Oh, great. Another question I don't know the answer to. I raised my hand again. Ms. Dobbins groaned at me and started walking my way. Why is she getting mad that

I'm asking questions? She should be *happy* that I care about my grades. "What is it now?" She asked.

"This question is asking what happened at the end, but I didn't see the end of the film."

"Well, I guess you shouldn't have been being a nuisance in my class." I lost it when she said that.

"I wasn't being a nuisance! You just overreacted!" I yelled at her. I didn't even care about being respectful at this point. The class said "ooh" at me. She looked at me in shock.

"Oh, really?" She said. I shrugged my shoulders.

"You're getting an F." She said, taking my paper. Are you kidding?! She's taking away my project because I threw facts in her face?! How mature.

"What why?!" I yelled. She ignored me and then went back to her desk. "Oh, and by the way, I'll be calling your mother today." She announced. A failing grade and a phone call home for what? Hurting her feelings?! Wait till they hear this one.

"Good, then she'll see that you gave me an *F* for no reason." I said, back. The class said "ooh" again and she looked at me in shock but didn't say anything. I put my head down on the desk. How could this day get any worse?!

After about 5 minutes, the phone rang. Ms. Dobbins picked up the phone.

"Hello? Yes, they're in my class .... Ok, I'll send them right now...." She hung up the phone and looked at me.

"Autumn, Zoey, Ivey. You're wanted at the principal's office." She said. Everyone started saying "ooh" again at the thought of me going to the principal's office. I rolled my eyes and started walking out of the class, but I was confused. Is this about Ivey pushing me?

Or did someone tell on Ivey and her friends for what they did to me in study hall? Only one way to find out, I guess.

We walked out the door and headed into the main office. Neither of us said a word to each other on the way there. Once we got there, we went to the principal's office and knocked on the door.

"Come in!" I heard him say. When we went inside Sandra, Tara and Leah were there too. I sat down in one of the seats in front of his desk.

"So, I wanted to talk to you about something. What happened between you and Ivey earlier?" He asked. I figured he was referring to what happened at Study Hall earlier. So long story short, I told the principal everything that happened in study hall between us.

"Ok, Ivey. Tell us your side of the story." Said the principal.

"Well, we were in class and Autumn kept humming to her music, so I politely asked her stop to at least 3 times, and then she got mad and started trash talking at us. So of course, we were firing back at her." Said Ivey. That's not what happened! Well, sort of, but most of that was watered down.

"Well, I don't know what this is about, but I was actually asking you guys what happened in the cafeteria earlier. But since you brought it up, let's talk about it." He said, confused. Oh, shoot! He didn't even know about what happened in Study Hall, he's talking about something else.

"So, based off of both of your stories, Zoey had nothing to do with any of this. Explain how Zoey ended up getting into this argument." He said to me.

"I don't know! She just randomly started screaming at me from across the room!" I said.

"That's not true! First off, she started staring at me, then waved. So, when I waved back, she told me to shut up." Said Zoey.

"What?! That doesn't even make sense. Why would I wave at you and then tell you to shut up?" I said.

"I don't know, it seems like you do a lot of things that don't make sense." She said. I rolled my eyes. I really hope he isn't buying any of this. Her story didn't even add up.

"Well, I still don't know what this is about, but I was actually asking you guys what happened in the cafeteria earlier. It's been brought to my attention that you threatened to hit Ivey?" He said. I was shocked. I never threatened Ivey! Well, I did mumble it to myself because she's irritating, but it's not like I said it *to* her.

"Wait, what? I never told Ivey I was going to hit her!" I said.

"Yes, you did!" Said Ivey. Right when she said that I felt like *actually* hitting her! Now, she's trying to get me in trouble with the principal to get revenge!

"No, I didn't!" I said back to her.

"Well, they're all saying that you did." Said the principal.

"But I didn't." I said again.

"They said you did." Said the principal. Seriously? "I didn't do it", "But they said you did." This sounds like a conversation between two little kids.

"Well, Yes, I did mumble it to myself because she was bothering me. But I didn't say it *to* her. I wasn't actually threatening her." I explained.

"Well, an indirect threat also counts as a threat." He explained.

I understood where he was coming from, but Ivey didn't really feel threatened by someone that she acts like is so insignificant. The only reason she and her friends told on me was so they could get revenge on me for telling the principal about everything they'd been putting me through all year. And I was stupid enough to give them a gun to shoot me with by falling into their tricks.

"I understand." I said.

"Now, I'd just like to ask, what is it about each other that you guys don't like so much?" He asked. Ivey and I both paused. Oh, I don't know. Maybe it's the fact that she's been *tormenting* me since I arrived here! Ivey raised her hand.

"Mind if I go first?" She asked, nervously.

"Sure, go right ahead." Said the principal. We turned to face each other.

"Autumn, I just want you to know that I actually *wanted* to be your friend for quite a while now. But you've just made it so difficult for me. You talk about me to your friends behind my back, you stole my boyfriend, and you've made me out to this mean girl, when really that's not who I am! I'm actually a really nice girl, but you'd never know that because you've never given me a chance...." She said.

I almost choked and fell out of my seat! That was pathetic! I'm not the reason for this beef we have! We wouldn't be fighting like this if she would just leave me alone and stopped telling people that I "stole her man". Her and Jackson weren't even dating! Get over it! And she hasn't tried being nice to me. The very first time I saw her at school, she and her friends were shooting me dirty looks because I talked to Jackson. So how is that trying to be nice?

"That's not the reason we don't get along. I don't get along with you because of how you've treated me since the day I arrived at this school! The first time I saw you, you were giving me dirty looks!" I said. Ivey gasped dramatically.

"I did no such thing!" She said. I rolled my eyes all the way into the back of my head. Is she for real? She's trying to play the victim card. Just then, the bell rang for school to be over.

"Ok, you're all dismissed." He said. We all started packing up our stuff so we could leave. They left before me. As I started to leave, the principal stopped me.

"Wait, Autumn. Before you leave...." He got out a piece of paper and started writing on it. Then he gave it to me. When I looked at it, IT WAS A DETENTION SLIP! I got a *detention* because Ivey told on me! I guess now I kind of see how she felt when I told on her, but I wasn't actually *harming* her!

"Detention?! I got a detention for what I said about Ivey?! I didn't even say it to her." I said.

"Yes, but it's still a verbal threat. And we have to take *all* threats seriously, direct or indirect. And the fact that you didn't say it to her face is pretty much what saved you from getting a suspension." Said the principal. My eyes nearly popped out of my head! They seriously thought about SUSPENDING me from school?! Is he being serious?!

"Now, just like it says on the slip, detention will be held in room 107 from the time school ends to 5:30. Be there no later than 3:30 or it may result in another detention or a suspension. Now, you can go ahead." He said. I got up and left his office.

When I walked outside of the main office, I saw Ivey still standing there, smiling at me with her arms crossed. I looked back at her with seriousness. We both stared at each other for a while now, then she looked me up and down, shrugged her shoulders and skipped away.

I couldn't believe I'd fallen into one of Ivey's tricks. She obviously was going to want revenge because I told on her. Why was I stupid enough to give her something? I guess this explains why she suddenly started acting nice in Ms. Dobbins' class. And now I still have to put up with their nonsense tomorrow, and the day after that, and then Friday is our last day before Christmas break. I started tearing up just thinking about the torment yet to come. And not only what's going to happen with Ivey, but I'm probably going to be in trouble with my mom because of my detention. I guess I'll just have to keep pushing through.

Since I still had about 25 minutes before detention started, I walked to the store that was next to the school and got a couple snacks. Then I went back to school to serve my detention time.

I got home at about 6:00, just in time for dinner. My mom was sitting on the couch. I put my book bag down and sat next to her. I'm probably in trouble for getting detention, so I treaded lightly.

"Hey, Mom." I said, nervously. She took a deep breath.

"Autumn, I'm going to ask you something and I need you to be completely honest with me." She said, without even looking at me. I got more nervous. "Ok." I said.

"Did you lie about Ivey pushing you into the classroom?" She asked. My eyes nearly popped out of my head and my heart dropped! How could my mom accuse me of *lying*?!

"What?! No! Oh, my gosh! How could you even ask me that?" I said.

"I knew it. My daughter is not a liar. Your principal sent me an email earlier saying that he thinks you're lying."

"Well I'm not!"

"Tell me what happened when he asked you."

"Well first off, me, Ivey and some other kids got called down to the office on the morning announcements. And he asked me what happened while Ivey and Zoey are standing *right there*! So, then he asks Ivey and all the kids is what I'm saying true, and everyone said they didn't see anything except for Serenity who said she heard someone say 'VIP comin' through' but she didn't see anything. And she mentioned a couple other physical incidents between me and Ivey. Meanwhile Ivey was standing there crying saying none of that is true and that both stories were lies." I explained. My mom paused and looked at me dumbfounded.

"So, you're telling me.... that he asked you and all of the other kids while she was right there.... and he's expecting them to be honest while she's there.... and she started crying because she was put on the spot...." Said Mom, trying to process what I was saying.

"Exactly!" I said.

"Ok...." She said. We sat there for a while.

"So, I heard you got detention today." Said Mom. I should've known *that* was coming. I looked down.

"Well, first off you're grounded." She said, matter of factually. Of course, I pretty much knew I was going to get in trouble. Even though it happened because of Ivey, it's still a detention.

"Second, what did you get detention for?" She asked.

"Well at lunch, Ivey was bothering me again, so I mumbled that I felt like hitting her sometimes, and someone heard me. So, I guess they wanted revenge on me for telling on Ivey earlier, so they went and told the principal on me. And when we got called down to the office, Ivey started up this big act saying how she really wants to be my friend but I'm too difficult and all this crazy stuff." I explained.

"Autumn, you still can't make threats toward people. If, God forbid, something ever *does* happen to her, they're going to suspect you first because of that threat you made. That's why schools have to take any and all threats seriously." She said.

"I understand, but Ivey just wanted revenge, she didn't really feel threatened."

"Of course, she didn't. But you still have to take responsibility for your actions. Just be more careful with your words."

One thing I need you to remember is that God will fight your battles. I told you before and The Bible says Vengeance is mine. You just have to give the problems over to God.

Mom, how do I give the problems to God? All you have to do is say Lord, I am tired of having to deal with these girls at school. I am doing my best not to react. But, I need you to take this problem away from me. And I now know that I cannot do this without you. I need your help. Autumn my sweet baby, you have to believe GOD will do it for you. You have to go back to school with the thoughts that its already done. When you see those girls, you just simply smile because you already know GOD is going to straighten it out for you. That's having faith.

"Ok, mom I will try it.

"Now, dinner will be ready in about 15 minutes. And until you're Christmas break starts, no phone, no tablets and you can have 30 minutes of TV, but that's it. For now, focus on your studies. Ok?" She said. I nodded. She got up and went into the kitchen.

I guess I have to take responsibility, but how could I be so stupid to fall into Ivey's trap? She *wanted* me to get in trouble because she was mad that I told the principal what she's been putting me through. I really don't know how much more of this I can take. But I am going to take my mom's advice and ask GOD to fix it for me. Its obvious the principal isn't doing anything effective to make it stop. Ivey and her friends and getting more and more angry with me as the days pass, Ms. Dobbins is back to *her* tricks and my mom just sending pointless emails back and forth with the principal isn't working either! It feels like I'm trying everything and everything's going wrong! Welp, when all else fails, let me try GOD. I only have 3 more days to go, and then Christmas break. I just have to keep holding on.

Chapter 19: The Clash

The next day, school just started off regularly, so let's skip ahead to 3rd period that day. When the bell rang, everyone ran to a seat.

"Ok, class. Today we're going to be working on these worksheets I'm about to hand out. It's front to back and it has 50 questions overall. Whatever you don't finish is homework." Said Ms. Dobbins. She started handing out the worksheets and we got to work.

After about halfway through class, I dropped my pencil. I tried to pick it up from where I was sitting, but then it rolled underneath of Ivey's desk! Uh, oh. Now what do I do? I decided I didn't want any confrontation, so instead I searched my pencil bag for another one. I had no pencils, but a bunch of pens, which Ms. Dobbins has some weirdly strict rule against. And if I ask Ivey to grab it for me, she'll probably just start bugging me again. So, I guess I have no choice but to try to get that pencil I dropped. I reached my foot as far as I could, but it wouldn't reach. I had to slouch my body pretty far into my chair so I could get it. But as I was reaching for it, my foot kicked the leg of her chair! And it was loud! She whipped her head around at me, and so did the rest of the class.

"Excuse me, I was just trying to grab my pencil and-" Ivey interrupted me.

"OH, MY GOSH! LEAVE ME ALONE!" She yelled, extremely loud! Keep in mind, this is in the middle of a quiet classroom, and she's screaming at me to the top of her lungs!

"It was an accident, chill." I said, nonchalantly. Suddenly, I saw Ms. Dobbins walking towards me.

You know that feeling when you're watching a horror film and someone is hiding from the killer and you can hear their footsteps approaching and the music is getting louder and then there's that sudden silence and no one knows what's about to happen? That's how I felt!

Once she got to my desk, my heart dropped into my stomach! You know there's a problem when you're feeling *this* type of anxiety because the teacher is walking toward your desk.

"Look, I'm sorry! I was just trying to get my pencil and she-" she cut me off.

"I don't care what happened. I'm so sick of you being in this class. You know why? Because it seems like there's always some type of trouble happening with you. Why can't you just act like a normal person and do your work without me having to come over here and tell you the same things over and over?! You're a selfish, arrogant nuisance and a troublemaker! And you wonder why people don't like you? It's no wonder they don't like you! You're immature, and you're depriving other kids of the education that they want with your nonsense. So, if you want to act like a little kid, go grab a pacifier, put your hair in pigtails and head on down to the pre-k across town. Because I'm tired of you and so are the other kids around you."

I couldn't believe she just said to that to me in front of the entire class again! I think we've been through this before and she apologized for the way she'd been treating me! I guess she only did that because the principal called her out on her craziness. She's a grown woman! And the reasons she said aren't the reasons why the other kids don't like me. They don't like me because *Ivey*, the most popular girl in school doesn't like me and the rest of them are just followers. And Ms. Dobbins.... I don't know what her problem is, but she seemed like she had a issue with me on my first day either! But either way, that's not her place to determine why or why not the other kids don't like me and it definitely isn't her place to announce something like that to a class packed with students. I don't get it, why do people always feel the need to "put me in my place" or completely shut me down by saying something extremely rude to me in order to get a point across, even if the situation isn't that serious? I'm a person just like them, and I want my education just like the other kids here. But NOOOO, they just *have* to make my middle school experience more difficult than it already is. Just let me live my life! Geesh!

Ms. Dobbins and I continued staring at each other. She was giving me the death stare, while I stared in shock. Out of nowhere, I heard someone laughing. I looked over and it was Zoey pointing at me laughing, as if to instigate.

"Don't laugh, Zoey. If you want to, you can join her." Said Ms. Dobbins, without even taking her eyes off of me. Zoey looked in shock and turned back around. I must admit, that took some of the pressure off of what she just said to me, just because she fired back at someone who was instigating. But I was still baffled by what just happened. As she started walking away, I finally spoke up. I'm tired of letting her get away with saying and doing whatever she wants to me. Teacher or not! She's not getting paid to like me, she's getting paid to teach me, so she should do *that* instead of insulting me any chance she gets.

"But- but that's not fair! You're a grown woman. You don't need to say things like that to a kid! I said I kicked her chair by accident and your reaction was completely unnecessary. Plus, whatever it is that you're holding onto, it's not my fault. You don't get to take your anger out on me, I'm 13!" I yelled back. The class said "ooh" quietly at me, as she whipped back around to face me. She and I both stared at each other for a while again. But this time, *she* looked shocked and I was giving the death stare.

"Go to the principal's office." She said, toughly, but quietly.

"Seriously? I-" she interrupted me, again.

"I SAID GO TO THE PRINCIPAL'S OFFICE! I don't want to see your face for the rest of the day." She said, pointing to the door. Glad we're both on the same page. I grabbed my stuff and headed out the door. When I was walking out of the door, I heard her mumble something and the entire class laughed. I rolled my eyes and walked faster down the hallway.

Once I got to the principal's office, I knocked on the door.

"Come in!" I heard him say. I opened the door and went inside.

"Autumn? Take a seat." He said. He seemed kind of surprised to see me, but sort of like he was expecting me. I sat down in the seat in front of his desk.

"So, Ms. Dobbins just called me not too long ago insisting that you get another detention because you were disrupting her class. Do you mind explaining what happened?" He said. Seriously? She insisted that I get a detention all because she's mad. And she calls *me* immature.

"What happened wasn't even that serious. I dropped my pencil behind Ivey's desk, and when I went to grab it, I accidentally kicked the back of her chair. Then, when I tried to apologize, she overreacted and screamed at me to leave her alone. So then, Ms. Dobbins came over to see what was up, so I tried explaining it to her, but she cut me off and went on this ridiculous tirade about how I'm such a selfish, arrogant nuisance and she's tired of me being in her class and if I want to act like a child to go to the pre-k across town. And when someone laughed, she told them that they could join me. So, I told her that it was an accident and that she was being dramatic and she doesn't need to take her anger out on me all the time, so she sent me out." I explained. The principal looked dumbfounded. I guess he was just as confused as me.

"Wait, so let's start from the beginning. You were reaching for your pencil and what happened?" He asked.

"And I accidentally kicked Ivey's chair." I said.

"Why didn't you just ask Ivey to grab it for you?" He asked. Why didn't I ask her? Why wouldn't you poke a grizzly bear with a stick?!

"Because I knew if I said something to her, it would spark a fight. So, either way, I'm the one getting in trouble."

"So, why did Ms. Dobbins get mad?"

"Exactly! She doesn't like me! It's hard being in a class where people don't like you no matter what you do."

"What do you mean?" I started tearing up a little bit again. Do you really understand how frustrating it is having to put up with the same thing every day over something that isn't even your fault?

"Since the day I arrived here, Ivey and her friends were giving me problems. I talked to Jackson *once* and that was it! All because I talked to a boy she liked; she's been tormenting me for this long. I've seen *SOOOO* many other problems in the world that could lead to a person despising another, but this girl is mad because someone *talked* to a *boy*! And on my first day in Ms. Dobbins class, when I told her about my accomplishments in science, she insulted me saying that I was probably in the delayed program or that I didn't have much competition. I've had quite a few teachers that are a little off in how they treat kids, but I don't think I've ever seen an adult as open about her dislike for a child as her. And I'm so sick and tired of having to put up with this amount of pressure and pain every day. Even at the previous schools that I've been to, I wasn't always the popular girl and I didn't always fit in that well. But so far, this school year has been one of my worst yet. Don't you understand how frustrating and annoying it is to have to put up with the same insults and the same type of people bothering you for this long?!"

Eventually I just broke down in tears. I'm glad I got my point across, but how many people are going to understand my situation? Do I even make sense? It makes me crazy sometimes just thinking about it!

The principal stayed quiet for a while, probably processing what he was about to say next. I hope he doesn't think I'm weird or crazy because of how I feel.

"Autumn, listen. You're not alone with how you're feeling. I've seen multiple incidents where the same type of stuff happens to you. In fact, when I was around your age, I ended up getting into fights because I looked at a girl that this guy liked. So, I understand where you're coming from. Kids can be really cruel and petty sometimes." He said. I nodded my head.

"Ok, you know what? I'm going to send you back to class." He said. I was sort of surprised. That's it? No lecture, no detention, nothing?

"Really?" I asked.

"Sure. Based off of what you just told me, I can't find any valid reason why you should have detention. All I have to say to you about it is to not talk back to a teacher. But I'll be talking to Ms. Dobbins today." He said.

"Ok, thanks." I said.

"You still have enough time to go to class, so go ahead to the bathroom for a couple minutes, straighten yourself up and go ahead back to class. Ok?" He said.

"Thanks, again!" I said, getting my stuff.

"No problem." He said. I left his office and went to the bathroom to go straighten up.

I wiped my tears and splashed some cold water on my face so my face wouldn't be so sticky. I'm sure some people still might be able to tell I was crying, but at least it wouldn't be that obvious. Once I was done, I started heading back to Ms. Dobbins' class.

Before I went inside, I took a deep breath and took a couple seconds to mentally prepare myself. Then I went in. Immediately when Ms. Dobbins saw me back, her eyes nearly popped out of her face!

"Autumn?! What are you doing back here? I thought I told you I didn't want to see your face for the rest of the day!" She yelled.

"Well, the principal couldn't find any valid reason to give me a detention, so he sent me back." I said, nonchalantly. Her nostrils flared up, and she started turning red again. She looked like she wanted to beat me up! I started heading back to my seat.

"OH NO YOU DON'T YOU LITTLE BRAT!" She yelled. I paused and turned back around to look at her. She was already up and out of her seating speed walking towards me. What, is she about to punch me in the face or something?

"GO SIT IN THE BACK!" She yelled, again. The back of the classroom? Again?! I thought she did that last time and she must've gotten in trouble considering she put me back in the front. But now she's back to it?!

"But I can't see from back th-" she interrupted me again.

"I DON'T CARE! You need to learn your lesson! That's going to be your seat until the end of the year! And I don't care what the principal says or does. You think the other kids in this class that start trouble got off the hook easy? No! And neither are you! You're no better than anyone here, so sit in that chair, where you belong, be quiet and act like a normal teenager! Got it?!" She yelled.

“But I never-“ she cut me off again.

“I SAID ‘GOT IT?!’” She screamed. I stood there for a second trying to process what had just happened. Is she seriously getting this angry at me because the principal refused to give me a detention over something as minor as the fact that she doesn’t like me? What is her problem with me? Why can’t she just treat me like anyone else in the class?

I let out a sigh.

“Ok.” I said. I didn’t want to talk back again and risk *actually* getting in trouble. So, I just went and sat in the seat she pointed to. Ms. Dobbins stared at me intensely for a couple of seconds, and then walked away to her desk.

I looked ahead and saw Ivey and Zoey looking back at me giggling again, like this is funny. I ignored them. I’m really not in the mood for their shenanigans. It’s been a long day already and it’s only 10:49! Oh, well. Just a couple more days and I won’t have to see these idiots until January.

After a while, the bell rang and everyone ran to their next period class.

Later that day at lunch, I was eating my lunch alone again when I saw something fly past my face and land on the table. It was a shoe! Boy, I’m so glad that didn’t hit me! Suddenly, I heard laughing in back of me. I didn’t even want to look back, because I knew it was Ivey and her stupid friends messing with me again.

“HEY! BRING ME MY SHOE BACK, LARDO!” Someone yelled. Then I heard more laughing. I didn’t want to get up and walk over there, because I knew they were probably just dying to start something if I do. Plus, I was already way too mad at them. So, instead I picked up the shoe, turned around and threw back at them. This time, it hit Ivey in the side of the head! Uh, oh! I’m *really* in for it now. I looked in shock, and so did Ivey. The rest of the table started saying "ooh" at us. Ivey looked at me with dismay. My heart sank into my stomach. What was about to happen? She jumped up out of her seat and began charging at me.

"DO YOU WANNA GO?!" She screamed. Leah ran and started pulling her back. I jumped up out of my seat too, to show her that I'm not afraid of her. Even though at that moment, I was terrified because I'd never been in a physical fight before.

"WHO DO YOU THINK YOU ARE?!" She screamed, again.

"Who do you think *YOU* are to throw things at me!" I yelled. By now, almost the entire cafeteria was watching to see what would happen next. Zoey, Sandra and Tara also started walking over to where we were standing.

"Just relax Ivey. It's not even worth her running and crying to the principal again." Said Leah, pulling her away from me. I don't know what it was, but as soon as she said that my forehead got hot and I couldn't even control myself! I guess I just got fed up with putting up with the same types of people for as long as I did.

"You know what?! I'm so tired of you guys tormenting me! If you guys don't like getting in trouble behind me then leave me alone! And the rest of you need to stop following behind whatever she says and does. It's not my fault-!"

Suddenly I got interrupted by a quick slap across my face! A hard slap! Everyone started saying "ooh" because someone hit me. I rubbed my face and looked up in shock. Ivey or one of her friends slapped me across the face while I was caught off guard!

"Maybe that'll teach you some manners." Said Ivey, getting closer to me.

I slapped her harder across the face. Everyone said "ooh" even louder. She looked at me in shock. I was sort of surprised I slapped someone too! But, when you have to put up with something that bothers you for this long, eventually you snap!

Pretty soon, her shock turned into anger, and she GRABBED ME BY THE NECK! As I tried to get her hands off, Leah, Zoey, Tara and Sandra started pulling on my hair and my clothes to make me fall. I wouldn't budge for a while, but after a few seconds, I fell. As I started getting up, I heard 2 more people running towards us! Oh, no don't tell me another person is here to help them.

"HEY! WHAT IS GOING ON OVER HERE?!" A voice screamed. Everyone paused in their tracks. I looked up and it was the lunch ladies. At least I know that they're here to break up the fight instead of instigating it. I looked around the room and started looking at facial expressions. Some of them were smiling like this is funny, some were of pure shock, and some were of fear. I looked at Serenity and Lauren and they were both shocked. I hesitated, but I looked at Jackson and Troy, too! They were both scared. Jackson sort of looked like he was about to do something but didn't. I looked back over at Ivey.

Ivey pointed at me.

"SHE STARTED IT!" She yelled. Oh, no. Now *I'm* about to get the blame for something that *she* started when she threw something at me! I pretty much already know how this cycle is going to go.

First; the lunch lady is going to send all of us to the principal's office, second; Ivey and her friends are going to lie and find some dumb excuse to say that I started the entire thing, third; the principal's going to do an entire investigation to get to the bottom of this, fourth; everyone is going to side with Ivey and I'll be the one getting in trouble with the principal, and last; Ivey is going to treat me even worse throughout the year and I'll have to keep coming back to the torment day after day.

Before anyone could say anything else, I got up and ran as fast as I could out of the cafeteria. I heard someone yell something at me as I was running out and then some people laughed, but I ignored them and ran faster.

I ran into the bathroom and looked at myself in the mirror. My clothes and my hair were messy from when they were pulling it, and I could see a big red mark from where I got slapped. I started to cry again, but before I could even think about the torment yet to come later, the door burst open! I looked and I was Ivey and her friends charging towards me again! How did they even get here so fast, especially since they were in the middle of a conversation with the lunch lady?!

"YOU'RE DONE, FREAK!" Yelled Ivey, pushing me to the ground. Before I could get up Leah went behind me and started dragging me by my hair while the other 4 started punching me in the face and body. I tried to start kicking and flailing my arms to get them off of me, but then Zoey held onto my arms so I couldn't. After a couple minutes of me freaking out, I somehow got out of her grasp and pushed her. Then, I started kicking again and got out of their grasp. I started storming away as all 5 of them stood up straight.

"YEAH! YOU'D BETTER RUN AWAY! You will never be welcome at this school!" Screamed Ivey, as I started running to the door. I pushed the door open and stormed out of the bathroom as fast as I could.

"Aww, is she going to cry?" I heard one of them say as I was exiting. Then I heard them laugh.

Once I was out of the bathroom, nearly 30-40 kids were standing outside listening! All in shock at what had just happened. I could only imagine how horrific I probably looked, especially after I had just gotten JUMPED! I didn't even stop to cry this time, I just wanted to leave the school after that. I ignored everyone looking at me and started making my way to the door at the end of the hallway.

After I'd made it past the crowd, someone came and tapped my shoulder. I was still jumpy, so it startled me a bit. It was Jackson. I don't know how I was supposed to be feeling, but I wasn't that happy to see him. What happened to "we can't be seen together anymore"? Why wouldn't he stand up for me when I needed it? Why would he wait till someone beat me up and then come and try to put his two cents in? We looked at each other for a couple seconds, and then I started storming off again. He stopped me again.

"Autumn, are you ok-?" I interrupted him. Do I *look* ok?!

"Stop! Just-" I started walking to the end of the hall again.

"Autumn, please-" I interrupted him again.

"Go away!"

"I just wanted to-"

"LEAVE ME ALONE!!!!" I screamed at the top of my lungs. He looked at me in shock. I was sort of shocked too at the fact that I screamed that loud, but I didn't care. I continued walking to the end of the hallway and walked straight out the door. I didn't care about getting in trouble either. I didn't know where I was going but all I knew was I didn't want to be there.

I ended up going home. I went inside, closed the door and threw my book bag onto the floor. My mom was in the living room playing with my baby sister Summer. She looked confused at the fact that I was home early but seemed even more shocked at how I looked.

"Autumn, what happened?!" She said.

"They beat me up! Look at me! I'm so sick of this!" I yelled, stomping upstairs. I went to my room, slammed the door, laid on my bed and cried.

Now, what am I going to do? It's like I'm afraid to turn any corner because Ivey and her friends would be there. All of my friends betrayed me, everyone in school thinks I'm a stuck-up brat who thinks I'm better than them, the principal isn't doing anything except making it worse and my mom's tactics aren't very affective either! I feel like I don't have any more fight left in me. Nothing is working. I don't know where to turn.

Eventually, my mom came in my room and sat down next to me. She sat there for a few minutes and didn't say anything. Pretty soon, she spoke up.

"Autumn, baby. Can you tell me what happened?" She asked. I took a couple seconds to calm down. Then, I wiped my tears, sat up and told her what happened. She looked at me in shock.

"Somebody put their hands on you again?!" She asked. I nodded.

"Ok, that's it!" She said, getting out her phone.

"What are you doing?" I asked, nervously.

"I'm calling the school and I'm going to see why they still haven't done anything about this!" She said.

"Mom! Don't you get it?! What you're doing is only making this worse! Here's how the cycle goes. You send pointless emails back and forth with the principal, the next day he gets me in his office and asks me about it, he says he'll handle it but instead just says something to Ivey to get her even more mad and then she'll keep treating me even worse because she knows that nothing is going to happen to her! Can't you see?! There's no stopping that girl! I don't know what to do, but the things you're doing aren't fixing it, you're making it worse." I explained. Mom stayed quiet for a while.

"So, you're just going to let them keep doing what they're doing to you?"

"No, it's not— Look, I don't know what I want to do, Mom. Nothing we're trying is working. I think we just need to move back Arizona."

"Look, Autumn. I really don't know what to say to you at this point. You're just giving up?"

"I don't know what else to do Mom! It's like everything we're trying just isn't working...." I paused for a second. I really didn't know what else to say.

"Can I just be left alone?" I asked. My mom looked a bit upset, but sort of like she understood.

"Ok. I'll let you cool off for a while. Just let me know if you need anything. And if you want to talk, I'm always here." She said. She started getting up to leave the room. I laid back down on my bed and buried my face in my pillow. After a few seconds, I heard her leave the room.

I laid there in my bed for a good while. No crying, just laying there. After a while, I thought about calling Troy when school was over, but then I remembered I'm still grounded, also because of Ivey. I seriously don't want to go back to school tomorrow. It makes me sick to my stomach just to think about the torment I was in store for. I just decided to not even think about it and get myself all worked up over it.

I must've drifted off for a while because I woke up to someone putting something on my dresser and then leaving the room. I looked at my alarm clock and it was 5:38pm! Well, there goes my sleep schedule, I guess. I looked on my dresser and I saw a big book. I got up and went to go see what it was and it was a Bible! I don't think I've read The Bible since we left Arizona! There was also a sticky note on the top of it. It said:

"Autumn, I don't have any other words to say to you except for read The Bible and pray about what you are going through. It's been a while since we've been to Church and gave some of our time to God. So, here is a list of Bible verses that you could read that could help you during this difficult time. Love, Mom."

I smiled. I felt kind of bad that I haven't been praying and reading The Bible as often as I should've been. I could definitely use it right now. I looked at the list and the first scripture listed was 2 Samuel 22:1-7. I picked up The Bible and read it.

After I read it, I felt encouraged, happy! Like there was hope that I was going to get through this. I decided to take it a step further by saying a prayer. I prayed and asked God to forgive me for my sins, and I asked Him to help me get through what I was going through with Ivey and her friends, Ms. Dobbins, everything that I was feeling was going wrong at the time.

After I finished, I felt relieved. God is just what I needed to help me through this journey.

Chapter 20: Worse Before It Gets Better

The next day at school, I wasn't as nervous as I had been throughout the week because I had this feeling that something was going to happen that would make my experience better. Other than dirty looks that I was getting from people in the hallway and some of my classes, everything seemed to be fine. Then, I got to fourth period. Let's just hope Ms. Dobbins doesn't act *too* crazy today.

I walked into the classroom and I didn't see Ms. Dobbins. I figured maybe she was just late to class or maybe she wasn't there that day. Oh, boy I hope she just isn't here today; I really don't feel like putting up with her today. Once the bell rang, everyone went to their seats and Ms. Dobbins still wasn't there. The rest of the class seemed just as confused as me, wondering where could she possibly be?

After about 2 minutes, the principal came in. Uh, oh. I hope this isn't about yesterday and that he's not here to make a big scene and start up an investigation in front of everyone and make Ivey or Ms. Dobbins hate me even more.

"Hello, everyone." He said.

"Hi!" The class said.

"So, I have some news for you guys. Your science teacher, Miss Karen Dobbins, will no longer be teaching with us. She's been transferred to our pre-k center located across town." Said the principal. Everyone gasped. I couldn't believe what I was hearing. Ms. Dobbins isn't teaching here anymore? Why? Does it have anything to do with me? Because I remember yesterday, she said something to *me* about going to the pre-k across town because I'm so immature.

"Yes, I know this is quite unexpected. But in the meantime, we'll be having a substitute teacher just for the rest of the week and then when you guys return from Christmas break, you'll have a new science teacher. Any questions?" He asked. One of the students raised their hand.

"Yes, William?" Said the principal.

"Why did she leave?" He asked. I was sort of wondering the same thing. Please don't be because of me!

"I'm really not supposed to give that type of information to students. But it doesn't have anything to do with any of you." Said the principal. I heard Ivey scoff. I looked in her direction and saw her mumbling something to Zoey. Then they both looked back and shot me a dirty look. I looked away and then they turned back around. Oh, boy. I really hope it wasn't because of her beef with me and the principal isn't just saying that to protect me.

"Any more questions?" Asked the principal. Nobody raised their hand.

"Ok, great. So, in the meantime your substitute will be here in a couple minutes. So, you guys can just work on these packets for the next two days. And the project you guys were working on while Ms. Dobbins was here is now exempt." Said the principal. Well, that's a relief! I would've gotten a zero on that project, thanks to Ms. Dobbins. He started handing out the packets and everyone got to work.

The next period, at lunch I sat down with my food. After about a couple of minutes, Ivey, Leah, Sandra, Zoey and Tara all walked up to my lunch table. Oh, no. What do they want now? I rolled my eyes.

"You must be so proud of yourself, aren't you?" Asked Ivey.

"What do you mean?" I asked.

"You know what I mean! You made Ms. Dobbins transfer!" Said Ivey.

"We don't know that was because of her problems with me. The principal said it didn't have anything to do with us." I said back.

"Principals have to say that to protect the student. But everyone knows you didn't like her and now all of a sudden, she just transfers after an argument with *you*? Don't think we're stupid, Autumn. You got that woman transferred." Said Leah.

"Or maybe she just set her over the edge so bad that she just asked to transfer." Said Zoey.

"Once again, we still don't know she transferred because of her problems with me. But either way it's not *my* fault she didn't like me." I said.

"OH, MY GOSH!" They all started yelling.

"We both know that you could've been less snobby if you tried, but NOOOO! You still wanted to walk around like you're the best thing since sliced bread!" Said Tara. By that time, almost half the cafeteria was watching, AGAIN!

"Why do you guys keep saying stuff like that? I don't think I'm better than everyone." Those are your thoughts, not mine.

"Well, good. Because clearly, you're not. I mean, look at those shoes. What are we, 4 years old?" Said Zoey. A bunch of people laughed at me, so I rolled my eyes at them.

"Would you guys just leave me alone and let me eat my lunch in peace?" I asked.

"Not until you admit that you were the one who got Ms. Dobbins transferred." Said Ivey. Finally, I heard someone else walk up behind me and speak up. It was Troy!

"Ivey, why don't you just leave her alone? Can't you see she's already been through a lot?" He asked.

"Oh, mind your own business Troy." Said Tara.

"Yeah, why are you standing up for *her*?" Asked Ivey.

"I'm standing up for a human being. A decent human being. You guys should really know your facts before you start talking about other people." Said Troy. Ivey and her friends looked at each other and laughed. Oh, my gosh! Thank God someone is finally stepping up to help me! But what he doesn't know is that I have someone who is always watching over me. Jackson, Serenity and Lauren started walking our way, too. I got excited for a second because I figured they were *finally* here to help me out a bit. Jackson came and stood next to Troy.

"Troy, don't." He Whispered. Troy gave him a sort of confused yet, dirty look and so did I! Why would he tell Troy not to stand up for me! What is his problem?! Is he really *that* worried about what Ivey thinks? I don't care, because I can stand up for myself.

"Why?" Troy asked.

"Yeah, Jackson! Why?" I said.

"If we keep standing around watching it happen, we're only letting it happen again and again." Said Troy.

"Look, just stop." Jackson said, again. I had pretty much lost my cool from there.

"What is your problem all of a sudden?! First, you ask me to the dance and now all of a sudden you're more worried about what *she* thinks than standing up for a friend?!" I said.

"I'm only doing this to protect you."

"No, you're only protecting yourself!"

"Look, there's just a lot going on right now."

"Oh, I'm sure there is. See, your problem is that after Ivey has been tormenting me for as long as she did, 'Mister I'm Too Cool For You' didn't want to ruin his reputation and now won't even talk to the girl he took to the dance because he's more worried about what a bully thinks!"

"That's not what's going on!"

"Then what is going on? Just tell me!"

"Autumn, calm down." Said Troy.

"I can't calm down! I NEED ANSWERS!" I yelled, on the verge of tears.

"AUTUMN!" Yelled Serenity. I looked at her. She kind of startled me. I stopped and looked around. Nearly everyone in the cafeteria was looking at me. I was so embarrassed that I went off like that in front of everyone. Suddenly, I heard Ivey giggling.

"Uh, did you seriously just do that?" Commented Lauren. Uh, oh. What now? I looked over at Ivey, and she was on her phone doing something.

"I sure did! Now everyone on the internet is going to see what a jerk you really are." Said Ivey.

Oh, my gosh! Again?! They're still back at it with taking videos of me! Didn't they get in trouble for something like that the last time? Do they just not know how to learn, or are they like that by choice? But I feel like I was even more mad at Jackson because he was the one that I was going off on, and he *still* wouldn't support me, even after something like this happened AGAIN.

I turned to face Jackson.

"Do you see why I'm so upset at you? As long as you sit there watching it happen, it's going to keep happening. I thought you cared about me." I said, my voice breaking. Jackson looked mad! Is he finally about to say something to Ivey?

"I don't need this." He said, storming off. Are you kidding me?! NOTHING!? Does he just not care about me? I was broken.

“What do you mean? And where are you going?” Asked Troy. Jackson ignored both of us and stormed out of the cafeteria. He really *does* hate me. Why did I ever trust this guy?

“As he should!” Zoey yelled out. The five of them started laughing again. Troy and I ignored them.

“I’m sorry, Autumn. I don’t know what‘s the matter with him all of a sudden. But in the meantime, you’ve always got a friend you can talk to when you need to.” Said Troy. I smiled at him.

“Thanks, Troy.” I said.

“Aww, look! The two dorks like each other.” Said Ivey. Everyone laughed again. Troy rolled his eyes.

“I’m going to go find Jackson and see what his problem is.” Said Troy. He left the cafeteria, too.

“Well, looks like we were right all along. Jackson *doesn’t* like you.“ Said Leah.

“I still can’t believe she actually thought for a second that she could tear me and my man apart.” Said Ivey.

“For the millionth time: you and Jackson were never a thing! You can’t just pick and choose who he can and can’t date.” I said, annoyed. The five of them started laughing at me.

“Oh, my gosh! She still doesn’t get it!” Said Tara.

“Jackson does not like you! Won’t you get that through your big head?” Said Zoey. Well, clearly Jackson didn’t like Ivey either. That’s pretty much the reason she’s mad at me. I was tired of arguing with them already, why won’t they just let me be?

“Just leave me alone.” I said.

“Look, now she realizes she’s wrong and she’s not going to say anything.” Said Ivey.

"Just leave this school! Nobody here even likes you. You have no friends, the teachers didn't like you and you even got a teacher transferred. You're just messing everything up! Just get out of here!" Said Zoey. Then the bell rang. Phew, saved by the bell.

"Come on, let's go." Said Ivey. They all flipped their hair at me and walked away. I rolled my eyes and headed to my next class. Nothing else really happened at school today besides that.

When I got home, I immediately went upstairs to my room and laid down on the bed. After what I'd just went through with Jackson, Ivey and the rest of them I didn't feel like doing anything.

I thought again about what happened with Ivey and her friends and I thought about Jackson, too. Why did I ever trust Jackson? I was so caught up in his looks that I forgot that guys like this are players. Now he won't even provide me with support when I really need it. Does he just not care about me? Did he not care about me from the start? Maybe Ivey and her friends were right earlier about Jackson hating me. I guess I should've just listened and not have gone to the dance with Jackson.

About 15 minutes later, I heard my mom calling for me. I groaned and started heading down the stairs to my mom. About halfway down the stairs, my mom looked up and jumped in fear.

"Oh, my gosh! You scared me. I didn't even see you when you came in. You were upstairs the whole time?" Said mom. I chuckled and came downstairs.

"Yeah. After the day I had, I didn't really feel like doing anything." I said. I sat down on the couch.

"Uh, oh. Another bad day?"

"Yep. But at least a couple good things happened."

"Well, let's talk about the good things that happened first." Said mom, sitting down next to me.

"Ok. Well, first off we found out that Ms. Dobbins got transferred to another school."

"That's good! You're making progress in your journey. See what happens when you pray and read The Bible?" I thought for a second. Come to think of it, right after I started back praying and reading The Bible, Ms. Dobbins was no longer a problem for me! That's pretty incredible if you ask me.

"Wow. I didn't even think of it that way." I said.

"Yep. Now, what other good things happened today?" Asked Mom.

"Well, I got into an argument with Ivey and her friends and Troy stood up for me. He was the only one out of my friends that didn't tell me that we couldn't be seen together anymore. Only I didn't realize he was still my friend until the day after Jackson, Serenity and Lauren betrayed me."

"See what God will do for you if you just trust Him?"

"I know, that *is* pretty cool how right after I prayed, my experience got a little better. But at the same time, it got worse."

"It got worse? How?"

"In the cafeteria, Ivey and her friends made this big scene about how I'm probably the one who got Ms. Dobbins transferred. So then when Troy came over to support me. Jackson came and tried to pull him away and stop him. So, I got mad and was asking him what his problem was and he said he was just doing it to 'protect' me. So, I started going off on Jackson and Ivey got the whole thing on video and posted it to the internet. AGAIN!"

"Wait, they put *another* video of you on their social media?"

"Yes. And don't try to send another pointless email to the principal, because in case you haven't noticed, the principal isn't doing anything about the videos, he's only making Ivey and her friends more and more angry at me."

"Ok, first of all watch your tone with me." Said Mom. I took a deep breath in an attempt to calm down a little bit.

"And second, I'm not going to send an email to the principal this time. All I'm going to encourage you to do is read The Bible and pray again. You noticed when you started praying your experience got better today, right?" Said Mom.

"Well, Yeah. But how come it got better *and* worse at the same time?" I asked.

"Well, Autumn. Sometimes the situation has to get worse before it gets any better. God works in mysterious ways, but in the end it's all part of His Plan. You just stay holding on and trust God will help you get through this. Ok?" Said mom. She gave me a hug.

"Ok." I said.

"Now, why don't you go ahead and get started on your homework for tonight." Said mom. I started heading upstairs to do my homework.

Later that evening around bedtime, I walked by my dresser with The Bible and list of scriptures on it. I decided if I was going to include God in my journey, I should be persistent and not make it just a one-time thing. God should be my steering wheel, not my spare tire. The second one on the list was Lamentations 3:13-25. I picked up The Bible and began reading.

After I finished reading, I decided to say a prayer before I went to bed. I prayed and asked God to forgive me for my wrongdoings, I thanked Him for the wondrous things He's done for me, and I asked Him to help me get through this last day of school before Christmas break.

After I finished, I went to bed. I was sort of excited since it was the last day of school before Christmas break and I felt hopeful that God was going to help me get through this.

Chapter 21: The Diner

My mom told me before I left for school that after school ends, I'm no longer grounded, so that's pretty cool! And other than getting weird looks from people in the hallway, nothing really crazy happened today. Plus, it was a half day, so it went by pretty fast. Let's just fast forward to the end of last period. As soon as the bell rang, everyone got up and ran as fast as they could out of the classroom into the hallway. And at one point, someone started streaming Christmas music on their portable speaker and everyone started dancing along. It was sort of like the last day of school, only Christmas themed. I didn't want to start any trouble, so I went straight to my locker to get my stuff and get the heck out of there.

When I was at my locker, two girls walked up to me. I got nervous for a second thinking it was Ivey or someone. But I looked and it was Serenity and Lauren! Uh oh, what did they want?

"Hey, Autumn." Said Serenity.

"Hey." I said, curtly. I tried to storm off again, but they stopped me.

"Wait, Autumn! We just wanted to talk to you about something." Said Lauren.

"What is it?" I asked.

"We just wanted to say we were sorry about how we'd been treating you this week." Said Serenity.

"Yeah, that was so wrong of us to leave you at your weakest point. That's not what real friends do." Said Lauren. I couldn't believe my ears! They're actually *apologizing*?! Or maybe, that's not what I heard. The Christmas music is so loud, I might have heard them wrong. I laughed.

"I'm sorry. For a second there, it sounded like you said you were sorry!" I said, yelling over the music. They both looked at each other, then back at me.

"We did." Said Serenity. I paused.

"Wait, what—" I stuttered. Oh, so *now* they want to be my friend again. What made them change their minds? I stopped and listened to them. But I don't trust them.

"Serenity and I talked again yesterday and seeing Ivey and her friends treat you even worse made us feel bad that we still weren't standing up for you. So, we tried calling your phone last night to apologize, but you didn't pick up." Said Lauren. Of course, I didn't! Because one; we weren't friends, and two; I was still grounded and my phone was turned off.

"And Autumn. I just wanted you to know that you have every right to be mad at us. We were horrible friends to you, and I won't even blame you if you don't want to be friends. But we just wanted to let you know that we've learned our lesson and that we're sorry for how we treated you." Said Serenity.

I stood there in shock. I couldn't believe it! They're actually apologizing! I don't know whether I should be their friend again or not. But then I remembered that The Bible says that you should have a forgiving heart. You never know; they might actually be sorry, and if I forgive them now, they'll probably be the best friends I could ask for. My decision was made. But I'm keeping my eyes on them.

"I forgive you guys." I said. They both paused and looked at each other, then back at me.

"Huh?!" They both said. I chuckled.

"I said I forgive you guys!" I said.

"Why?" Said Serenity. Lauren and I both looked at her.

"Well, I mean thanks for forgiving us, but why?" She said, again.

"Because.... with all of this stuff happening, I decided to bring my struggles to God. And He's been bringing me back on the right track. And, I should have a forgiving heart just like He does!" I explained. They both smiled.

"That's really good for you, Autumn!" Said Lauren.

"Yeah!" Said Serenity. Wow, I'm glad my friends are being encouraging to me in my faith. You don't find that many friends like that anymore.

"So, are we good?" I asked. They smiled again.

"Of course!" Said Serenity. The three of us hugged. After the three of us stopped hugging, I heard one of my favorite Christmas songs playing.

"You guys wanna dance?" Asked Serenity.

"Is that even a question?" I asked. The three of us laughed, jumped into the crowd and danced to the Christmas music.

After about 10 minutes of us dancing, teachers started coming out of classrooms and telling us to leave, so everyone started leaving the school.

"Oh, my gosh. I'm starving." Said Serenity.

"Same." I said.

"You guys wanna go to the diner for lunch? It's not too far from school, we can literally walk from here." Said Lauren.

"Yeah! Let's go." Said Serenity.

"Hold on. Let me text my mom first. I don't want her to have a freak attack because I'm not home on time." I said. The three of us chuckled. I started texting my mom. Here's how the conversation went:

“Hey, Mom! Is it ok if I went to the diner with Serenity and Lauren for lunch?”

“Serenity and Lauren? I thought you guys weren’t friends anymore.”

“We made up.”

“Wow! See what God will do for you? Just keep trusting Him. We will talk later, but in the meantime you can go.”

“Thanks mom!”

Serenity and Lauren were still waiting for me.

“She said I could go!” I said.

“Great, let’s go.” Said Serenity. We started heading to the diner. It really wasn’t that far a walk; it took about 5 minutes to get there.

Once we got there, we sat down.

“So, who’s excited about the Christmas party tomorrow?” Asked Serenity.

“I know I am! I already picked out my outfit.” Said Lauren.

“I wasn’t really planning on going.” I said.

“Why not?” Asked Lauren.

“Well, since we weren’t talking to each other at the time, who would I go with?” I said. Serenity and Lauren both looked embarrassed.

“Oh, right.” Said Lauren.

“It’s fine. But do you guys think I should go now?” I asked.

“Of course! It’s a Christmas party!” Said Serenity. The three of us laughed.

"Alright, then I guess I'll check with my mom when I get home and see if I can go." I said.

"Yay!" They both said. We giggled. After about 45 minutes, after we were just finishing up our food, we decided to just talk and catch up for a while. Suddenly Serenity, who was on her phone, looked shocked and gasped.

"What happened?" I asked.

"You won't believe what just happened with Ivey and her social media account." Said Serenity. Oh, no. Now what? Why can't we just have a peaceful, stress-free Christmas break? Serenity showed Lauren her phone. Lauren gasped too.

"What is it?! The suspense is killing me!" I said.

"IVEY'S ACCOUNT IS SHUT DOWN!" They both yelled. I couldn't believe my ears!

"What?!" I yelled. Serenity showed me her phone and it was true!

"Oh, my gosh! What happened?!" I yelled.

"I don't know, but her account is temporarily suspended." Said Serenity. I was confused, but I was happy and relieved at the same time! That means people can't see the videos she posted of me anymore! But why is it shut down? Still, it's great that I don't have to put up with Ivey's cyber bullying for a while.

"Let's just not worry about it. Instead, let's celebrate! At least people can't see the videos for now." Said Lauren.

"You're probably right. Who's up for milkshakes?" Said Serenity.

"Me!" Said Lauren and I. When the waiter came back, we ordered some milkshakes as a celebration. But the three of us were left wondering why her account was suspended. I got home at about 2:30 and my mom was in the living room waiting for me.

"Hi, sweetie! How was it today?" She asked.

"I actually had a lot of fun. And you won't believe what happened at the diner today!" I said.

"I'll get to that in a minute. But first, let's talk about what happened with you, Serenity and Lauren. How did you guys make up so fast?"

"Well, I was at my locker getting ready to leave and they approached me and said that after what happened yesterday with Ivey and Jackson, they felt bad for the way they treated me throughout the week. Then, admitted that it was wrong of them to leave me at my hardest time. And I accepted their apology because I realized that I should have a forgiving heart just like God does." I said. My mom smiled at me.

"Look at you being the bigger person! I'm so proud of you...." Said mom, hugging me. I smiled.

"And I hope now you see what I was saying yesterday about how sometimes the situation has to get worse before it gets better. Notice how after something bad happened, Serenity and Lauren realized they were wrong and apologized to you." Said mom.

That was actually a really good point. I was confused before because right after I prayed and read The Bible, Ivey posted *another* video of me. And then the next day, after I prayed and read The Bible I made up with my friends *and* Ivey's account got temporarily disabled. God really *does* work in mysterious ways, but it's all part of His Plan.

"Wow, I guess you were right, Mom!" I said. Mom smiled.

"Now, tell me what happened at the diner." Said Mom.

"Serenity was scrolling through her social media and she saw that Ivey's account has been temporarily disabled!" I said.

"Wow!" Said Mom.

"Now people can't see those videos she posted of me for a while. But even if the system does let her back on, I don't know if the videos will still be there." I said.

"Wow, two good things in one day. See what prayer can do?"

"I know! And guess what else."

"There's more?"

"Yep! Serenity and Lauren are going to the Christmas party tomorrow."

"Christmas party?"

"Oh, yeah. I don't think I told you. The school is having a Christmas party tomorrow in the library. Is it ok if I go?"

"What time is the party and how long is it? I don't want you out too late."

"It's tomorrow from 5-9 in the library."

"Well, I suppose if you want to, you can go."

"Yay!" I said. My mom chuckled.

That evening, after I had done my night time routine, I decided to read The Bible and pray again. Next on the list was Psalms 27. After I finished reading, I said a prayer.

I prayed and asked God to forgive me for my sins. I thanked Him for allowing me to make up with my friends and for what happened with the video of me on Ivey's social media. Then, I prayed and asked Him to allow me to have a good time at the Christmas party the next day.

After I said my prayer and read The Bible, I decided to just relax for the rest of the evening.

Chapter 22: The Christmas Party

The next day, around 4:30, I started getting ready for the Christmas party later on. I wanted to go for a Christmas-y and formal, but approachable look. So, I decided to wear my red and white Santa-style dress, with some white flats and I wore my red and white necklace with some Christmas ornament earrings. I was just finishing up doing my hair when my mom walked in.

"Autumn, are you almost ready?" She asked.

"Not yet. I just have to put the finishing touches on my look." I said.

"Well, I hope you have fun today." Said mom.

"I hope so too. But I'm kind of worried." I said.

"About what?"

"What if something bad happens at the Christmas party, too? Like what if Ivey shows up and does something to embarrass me just like at the dance?"

"Don't worry about that. Just have a good time with your friends."

"I know, but what if?"

"Well, if you feel that way, say a prayer before you go. Just have a good time and don't worry about drama."

"I guess you're right." I said. I finished doing my hair and I was ready.

"Ready to go?" Asked mom.

"Yep." I said. My mom and I both exited my room and started heading downstairs. My little sisters and my dad were downstairs waiting for me.

"You have a good time, Autumn." Said Dad.

"Thanks, Dad!" I said.

"Why couldn't I go with you? That's not fair!" Said Nikki.

"Nikki, it's a middle school party. And plus, your school already had a party for you guys." Said mom.

"It was in the middle of the school day, they passed around Christmas cookies and played one Christmas song. That doesn't count." Said Nikki. We chuckled.

"We should start heading out! We don't want to be too late." Said Mom.

"Ok, let's go." I said.

"Wait. If you see that jerk Jackson there, let him know I said—" My mom interrupted my dad.

"Whatever you're about to say, don't say it in front of the little ones." She said. My dad leaned closer to me.

"I'll just text you." He whispered. I chuckled and rolled my eyes.

"Ok, I'll see you guys later! Bye!" I said.

"Bye!" Everyone said. My mom and I walked out the door, got in the car and drove to the school. I said a prayer on the way to the school. I asked God to forgive me for my sins, I thanked Him for the wonderful things that He's already done for me and I asked Him to help me have a good time with my friends at the party.

We arrived at the school at around 5:15.

"Alright, now you have a good time. And remember what I told you!" Said mom.

"Ok, see you later mom!" I said, getting out of the car.

"Bye!" She said. I closed the door and my mom pulled off.

I went inside the school and there were Christmas decorations all throughout the hallway. But when I went inside the library, there were even more decorations. There were candy canes hanging up everywhere, they had a big Christmas tree, there was Christmas music playing and the room smelled like gingerbread! I even saw someone dressed up as Santa Clause taking pictures with people. It was amazing!

Eventually, I saw Serenity and Lauren walking up to me excitedly. Serenity had on reindeer antlers and they were both wearing ugly Christmas sweaters with jeans.

"Hey, Autumn!" Said Serenity.

"Hey, guys! I like your outfits." I said.

"Thanks! I like yours too. It's so Christmas-y." Said Lauren.

"Thanks. I was going for a dressy, but approachable look." I said.

"Looks like they went all out for Christmas this year!" Said Lauren.

"I guess they pretty much had to, especially after the lame Halloween party they threw. I could've thrown a better party than that!" Said Serenity. The three of us chuckled. Pretty soon, another song started playing.

"Wanna go dance?" Asked Serenity.

"Sure!" Said Lauren and I. We hopped into the crowd and started dancing.

We ended up having a lot of fun! We danced to the music, ate some Christmas cookies, drank eggnog, and even took some pictures together with Santa Clause! I was hardly even thinking about Jackson or Ivey.

After about an hour and a half, as we were dancing, I heard someone running towards us.

“HEY!” They yelled, pushing me to the ground! Everyone stopped and looked. I looked up and it was Ivey and her friends! My heart dropped as soon as I saw her standing over me. What did she want now? Can’t we just have a peaceful day?

“How dare you push me!” I yelled, starting to get up. Serenity and Lauren helped me stand up. I charged towards her but Serenity pulled me back.

“Yeah, what is your problem?” Asked Serenity.

“My problem is that this little snitch got my social media suspended! She reported me for ‘harassment’! And don’t even try to deny it. You snitched on me before, why wouldn’t you snitch now?” Said Ivey. I had a pretty good feeling she was going to show up wanting to start something, but how dare she make a big scene in front of everyone! I don’t even know how her account got suspended!

“No, I didn’t! I don’t even have social media!” I said.

“Oh, don’t play stupid! I’m so sick and tired of you in this school. Things would be so much better around here if it weren’t for you!” Said Ivey.

“Exactly! And she still continues to walk around the school thinking she’s better than everyone here. No one likes you, just get out of here!” Said Leah. I was pretty much speechless at this point. What I do know it that I wasn’t the one who reported her. I didn’t even know what happened or even who reported her.

“Don’t listen to her, Autumn. We do want you here.” Said Lauren. I smiled at her.

“Oh, don’t lie to her. You probably don’t want her here either.” Said Tara.

"That's enough out of you guys. You've put her through enough, and we're tired of sitting back watching you guys torment her all because Ivey's jealous." Said Serenity. The five of them busted out laughing.

"Me? Jealous of *her*? You're delusional." Said Ivey.

"Oh, don't play dumb. You didn't like Autumn from the get-go. And it all started after she talked to Jackson *once*!" Said Serenity.

"And I gave her a warning then, and she still continued to test my limits. She needs to be put in her place." Said Ivey.

"Ivey, you're ridiculous—" Ivey interrupted me.

"I don't even want to hear you speaking! First, you steal my boyfriend, then you get me in trouble with the principal, and now you even got my social media disabled! You're out of control!" Said Ivey.

"That's it! Enough is enough." Someone else said. I looked behind me and it was Troy!

"What did you just say?" Said Ivey, as if to threaten him.

"I said enough is enough. You're the one that's out of control. You're seriously causing this big scene and we're just trying to have a good time." He said.

"And we could go back to having a good time if Autumn would just admit that she was the one who got my account suspended and then leave." Said Ivey.

"She's not the one causing the trouble, you are!" Said Serenity.

"I will leave her alone when she tells everyone the truth!" Said Ivey.

"I didn't!" I said. Now get out my face.

"Well, someone had to!" Said Leah.

"I did." Another voice said. I looked behind me again and I couldn't believe what I was seeing.... It was Jackson! But how? Why? I had so many questions. Everyone else seemed like they were just as shocked as me!

"Jackson?! How could you?" Said Ivey.

"Because I'm sick of the way you've been treating Autumn, too. And not only that, but the amount of lies that you've told about Autumn *and* about me!" Said Jackson. Ivey looked sort of nervous.

"What are you talking about?" She asked.

"First of all, let's talk about that lie you spread around that we were dating when we actually weren't!" Said Jackson. I was completely shocked! *I* knew that they weren't dating, but I definitely wasn't expecting Jackson to say something like that in front of everyone! Everyone gasped, and slightly giggled.

"Jackson, you don't have to pretend for her. She's nobody!" Said Ivey. I rolled my eyes.

"Ivey, we both know the truth. It's time you started accepting it." He said back to her, slightly quieter. By now, the entire party was watching, silently waiting for something else to happen. Ivey looked at me with pure anger in her eyes. My heart sank again. What is she about to do?

"I BLAME YOU!" She yelled, charging at me, but then her friends held her back.

"LET GO OF ME!" She screamed.

"That's enough of that." Said Jackson. My heart fluttered. He's finally standing up for me! But why? What happened? Ivey looked shocked, too. She broke free of her friends' grasp but didn't charge at me this time.

"Don't you see what she's doing! She's turning all of you against me!" Said Ivey.

"I don't think we needed Autumn coming here to see what a mean-hearted bully you are." Said Jackson. Everyone started saying "ooh" and giggling at his comment.

Ivey's nostrils flared up and her face turned red. She started looking around at people to see who would side with her, but it seemed like the only people on her side at this point was her friends. She groaned loudly and angrily, then stormed out of the party. Tara, Leah, Zoey and Sandra followed behind her.

I'm still trying to process what just happened here. Am I imagining this? What the heck is going on? I thought Jackson hated me! I guess everyone else was just as confused as me, because everyone else was murmuring with pretty much the same expression on their face as me. Jackson started looking around, too.

"You guys, just let me say this." Said Jackson. Everyone got quiet.

"I know I should've cleared this up sooner.... but Ivey and I never dated." He said. Everyone gasped.

"That's just a rumor that she would spread around just so no one would date me. And it's not Autumn's fault we weren't together. She was just jealous because she knew what I saw in Autumn, and she couldn't handle it." Explained Jackson.

In a way, I was really touched and shocked by Jackson doing what he just did in front of everyone, but I was still sort of mad at him and confused. Why act like this now, but when I was at my weakest point, he wanted nothing to do with me?

Jackson started walking up to me. I didn't know what to say or do at this point. Should I thank him? Should I cry? Should I get mad? Should I walk away? What do I do?

"Ok. I know you're probably mad at me right now, and maybe even a little bit confused." He said. I chuckled.

"Yes, I'm very confused actually." I said. He chuckled awkwardly.

"Just.... Why? Why are you being so nice now, but before you seemed like you wanted nothing to do with me?" I asked.

"Look, I'm so sorry for all of that. But, as I was saying before, I was only doing it to protect you.... That night at the dance, after Ivey humiliated you like that in front of everyone, I saw how upset you were, and I felt terrible. I felt like I could've prevented it from happening, but I failed. And I felt even worse knowing that Ivey would've probably left you alone if *I'd* left you alone. So, I figured if I stopped talking to you then Ivey would get what she wanted and stop bothering you. But it turns out it had only gotten worse from there. First, Troy told me about what happened between you, Ivey and her friends in study hall and how much you cried. But then when I saw Ivey and her friends trying to beat you up that day, I was on edge throughout Thursday, the day you and I got into that fight. Finally, when I saw Ivey post *another* video of you right in front of me, I couldn't take it anymore. I couldn't even stand being there, so that's why I left. That day was my final straw, so I reported both videos she took of you that were on her social media, and the next day I saw that her account was suspended." He explained.

As he was saying all of this, I was in awe. He really did all that because he thought it would keep Ivey from bothering me? I took a couple seconds, and then started talking.

"So.... you did all of that just to keep Ivey from bothering me?"

"It may not have been the wisest choice, but I didn't know what else to do." I stared into his eyes again, it felt like the moment we first made eye contact all over again, just like how I felt at the dance. My heart started beating super-fast again and I felt at least a million butterflies. Is this what love feels like?

"And....if you're still mad at me, I don't even blame you. I didn't even let you know what was going on. I just told you out of the blue that I couldn't be seen with you anymore. I just didn't know how to tell you. But I did know that I didn't want to see you get hurt anymore." Said Jackson.

I don't know what came over me, but suddenly I felt myself walking forward, and I kissed Jackson right on the lips! He kissed me back! When we pulled away, I was shocked at myself. I just had my first kiss! I didn't even know I had that type of game. But I guess I did. Jackson and I smiled at each other.

"So, does that mean you forgive me?" He asked, smiling. I giggled.

"Of course, it does." I said. We continued smiling at each other.

Eventually, we heard clapping and cheering. I had almost forgotten everyone was there! It felt like it was just Jackson and I in the room for a second there. I looked around and everyone was cheering us on. Jackson and I looked back at each other and smiled.

"So.... are we like.... a thing now?" Asked Jackson.

"I don't know, are we?" I asked. Before Jackson could even answer my question, we heard someone yelling. We both looked and it was Ivey storming back into the library. Oh, no! Now what?! Can't we just have a happy ending and leave it at that?

She came and stood in the middle where Jackson and I were.

"Ivey, whatever you're about to do just give it up. You lost!" Said Serenity.

"I only came back here to let you all know that I'm over Jackson, and I have someone else in mind." Said Ivey. Everyone was surprised. She's over Jackson that quickly? I mean, that's good for me, but who else could she have in mind?

"Already? Who?" Asked Lauren. Ivey walked over to Troy.

"It's Troy!" She said. Everyone gasped. Troy looked even more shocked. Seriously? Jackson's best friend? Talk about petty!

"So, what do you say, Troy? Wanna get out of here and get something to eat?" Said Ivey, shamelessly flirting. I rolled my eyes as far back as they could go.

Troy has a crush on Ivey! It's pretty obvious that he's going to say yes. But how will Jackson react if they end up going out? Will Jackson end up getting jealous and realize he likes Ivey more than me? I looked up at Jackson, and in fact he didn't even look that surprised. I looked back at Troy to see what his answer would be, even though I'm sort of expecting him to say yes. By now, everyone was quietly waiting for something else to happen.

Troy paused for a second, then looked back at Ivey.

"No." He said, straightforward. Everyone, including me, Ivey, and Jackson, gasped and looked in pure shock! What did he mean "no"? I thought he liked Ivey!

"No?! What do you mean no? Don't tell me you like Autumn, too." Said Ivey.

Uh, oh. I hope the reason Troy rejected Ivey wasn't because of me. How would that affect his friendship with Jackson? How would it affect his friendship with me? And would it affect my relationship with Jackson?

"It's not because of Autumn." He said. I let out a sigh. That's a relief. But why did he reject Ivey, too?

"Then why don't you want to date me?" Asked Ivey. Troy paused for a couple seconds.

"Ok, I'm going to be honest. You're hot." He said. Ivey flipped her hair and some people chuckled. I rolled my eyes.

"But just because you're pretty on the outside, doesn't mean you're pretty on the inside. You only want to date me to make Jackson jealous again, just like last time before the dance. You only asked me out to make Jackson jealous before. And it didn't work last time, so why try it now? And besides, I'm not about to throw away years worth of friendship over a girl." Said Troy. Everyone started applauding for him. Ivey started looking around to see if anyone would side with her again. I guess she still didn't see anybody.

"You know what? I don't need you people! I'm out of here." She said, storming out again.

"Don't let the door hit you on the way out!" Said Serenity, as she left. Everyone started laughing. Ivey left the library and slammed the door shut. Eventually, the music came back on and everyone started dancing again.

"You wanna dance?" Asked Jackson. I smiled at him.

"Of course!" I said. Jackson, Troy, Serenity, Lauren and I all danced to the Christmas music and enjoyed the rest of the party.

Wow, what a week! I still can't believe how far I came. I went from being completely hopeless and alone to being happy and dancing with my friends. I guess that's what prayer can do. Think about it, before I started back praying and reading The Bible, the situation was completely hopeless. But the minute I started back, everything started picking up. At first, it started off a bit rocky, but The Lord works in mysterious ways. Who would've thought what I went through on Thursday with Ivey and Jackson would've actually paid off later? I guess the situation really does have to get worse before it gets better sometimes. I just couldn't lose faith, and I had to keep trusting that God would help me, and He did! Where would I be if I didn't start praying and reading The Bible again? I guess, this is a great example of the power of prayer.

Epilogue

It is now mid-July and so much has happened throughout the year. So, let's just do a quick recap. Throughout the year, Ivey was still mad at Jackson and I because of what happened at the Christmas party, but at least she hasn't given us any big problems besides giving us dirty looks when she sees either one of us. But neither of us really care what she thinks. When Ivey got her social media account back, both videos of me that she posted were gone! Plus, we ended up getting a new science teacher, too! Not only is he a great teacher, but he's super fun! He even let me retake the test Ms. Dobbins failed me on because she says she heard talking on my side of the class. I ended up getting a 95% on it! So, my final grades this year were straight A's and two B's. And even later in the year, we ended up finding out the real reason Ms. Dobbins got transferred was because the new school she works at now is closer to where she lives. But Ivey still thinks she left because of me. Also, did I mention that Jackson and I are an item? Yep! We made it officially official on January 18. And we've been going together ever since.

Throughout the end of the school year and the beginning of summer break, tensions were really high because we're about to enter high school! I heard high school is a lot of work and a lot of pressure, so we're all really nervous. So, to ease tensions and take the stress off of us, my family and I would plan little fun days for us and let us swim in the lake together! Serenity, Lauren and I were at each other's houses almost every day! Jackson and I would visit each other sometimes too, but we were mostly at his house because my dad's a snooper. I guess I was also right earlier about having a forgiving heart! Ever since I forgave Serenity, Lauren and Jackson for betraying me, they became the best friends I could ever ask for!

What I was really surprised and excited about was when I found out that Serenity, Lauren, Jackson and Troy were all Christians, just like me! Now we can talk to each other about our faith and the struggles that we're going through together. I almost couldn't be happier.

I also learned an important lesson this school year that I won't soon forget; the power of prayer! It was incredible the type of stuff that I accomplished just by putting my trust in God. My situation almost seemed impossible to get out of, but all I had to do was keep trusting that God could help me, and He did! So, my advice to you; trust God. Have faith in Him and He'll surprise you! Even when the situation seems like it's hopeless or it's getting worse, you'll make it out eventually, so just keep holding on. So, with this conclusion, I hope you now understand that I am a living witness of the power of prayer.

The end

Made in the USA
Middletown, DE
29 October 2020